THE GIFT IS IN THE MAKING

THE GIFT IS IN THE MAKING

ANISHINAABEG STORIES

RETOLD BY LEANNE SIMPSON

**ILLUSTRATIONS
BY AMANDA STRONG**

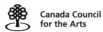
Canada Council
for the Arts

We acknowledge the support of the Canada Council for the Arts, which last year invested $153 million to bring the arts to Canadians throughout the country.

Nous remercions le Conseil des arts du Canada de son soutien. L'an dernier, le Conseil a investi 153 millions de dollars pour mettre de l'art dans la vie des Canadiennes et des Canadiens de tout le pays.

HighWater Press acknowledges the financial support of the Province of Manitoba through the Department of Sport, Culture & Heritage and the Manitoba Book Publishing Tax Credit, and the Government of Canada through the Canada Book Fund (CBF), for our publishing activities.

HighWater Press is an imprint of Portage & Main Press

Illustrations by Amanda Strong
Cover and interior design by Relish New Brand Experience
Printed and bound in Canada by Friesens

This book is also available in electronic format. See www.highwaterpress.com

Library and Archives Canada Cataloguing in Publication

Simpson, Leanne, 1971-, author
    The gift is in the making : Anishinaabeg stories / retold
by Leanne Simpson ; illustrations by Amanda Strong.

"This collection is a retelling of previously published, traditional
    Nishnaabeg stories, with the exception of 'Good neighbours'".
Includes bibliographical references.
Issued in print and electronic formats.
Includes some words in Nishnaabemowin.
ISBN 978-1-55379-376-2 (pbk.).-- ISBN 978-1-55379-381-6 (pdf)

20 19 18 17   4 5 6 7 8

    I. Strong, Amanda, 1984-, illustrator II. Title.
III. Title: Anishinaabeg stories.

PS8637.I4865G54 2013   jC813>.6   C2013-902719-X
                                                C2013-902720-3

THE DEBWE SERIES
Exceptional Indigenous writing from across Canada

HIGHWATER
PRESS

100–318 McDermot Ave.
Winnipeg, MB Canada R3A 0A2
Toll-free: 1-800-667-9673
www.highwaterpress.com

To all the Nishnaabeg families that keep lighting the Seventh Fire, each time it gets blown out, and to ndaankoobjignag.

CONTENTS

Kipimoojikewin: The Things We Carry with Us

When my children were born, I wanted to bathe them in the oral traditions of the Nishnaabeg so they would grow up grounded in their own sense of being and take their space in a world often intent on erasing Indigenous peoples. I wanted the beauty of Nishnaabeg culture to protect them from the harshness that is so often our reality. I wanted to wrap them in a blanket of stories they could carry with them through their lives and pass on to their own children and grandchildren. I wanted these stories to be part of their inheritance, their kipimoojikewin, the things we carry with us. So, in the same way that the many generations of Nishnaabeg parents who have come before me have done, I started telling them stories. At first, they were funny narratives about our family. These grew into teachings about creation and origin, then became stories about how to live a good life, and finally became narratives of resistance and resurgence. But, soon, I ran out of stories, and I began actively seeking them out from Elders, from other storytellers, and from written sources. After a few years, my children were telling these stories back to me; it was clear that they were noticing the concepts and the narratives in the landscape and in the fabric of their lives.

Pretty soon, two Nishnaabeg women in my community noticed what I was doing, and they asked me to tell these stories to larger groups of people. At first I was terrified, never having considered myself a storyteller. They laughed, saying, "But you're always telling stories; just tell some of those." Then, an Elder in our community reminded me—as our Elders so often do—"If you don't take this on, who will?"

The stories in *The Gift Is in the Making* began as part of a larger, oral, body of work, first told to my children over the last decade and then over the course of a year to a small group of families in an Nishnaabemowin language nest in Peterborough, Ontario, called Wii-Kendiming Nishinaabemowin Saswaansing, The Art of Learning the Language in the Little Nest. As a collective, we were looking for a fun and gentle way to connect our children to our land and waters, our language and oral literature. Over the year, language teacher Vera Bell translated the stories back into Nishnaabemowin as I told them in English; in my mind this is the very best way to hear our stories—that is, orally and in the language. Because of this, my original intent was to write down only the skeletons of these narratives, which families could use as reminders for telling them in their own way at home, because I believe the very best way to tell these stories is orally. I am hopeful that this book can be used as a tool to regenerate our culture and our nation.

At a most basic level, the stories in this collection teach both individuals and collectives how to promote, nurture, and maintain good relationships, how to function within a community, how to relate to the land, how to make collective decisions, and how to be a good person—that is, by being true to our traditions. They do so in a way that doesn't feel like learning. On a deeper, conceptual, level, they teach about Nishnaabeg political culture, governance and diplomacy, decision making and leadership. They carry within them our political traditions and our most deeply held collective values. Nishnaabeg systems of governance begin at home with stories like the ones in this book, and it is the responsibility of storytellers to plant them, like seeds, inside the minds and hearts of our children, with the hope that, under the right conditions, the stories grow and flourish as the next generation carries them through their lives, and then passes the seeds along to the next.

Storytelling within Nishnaabeg traditions is a wonderful way of teaching and inspiring not only children but also people of all ages. Young children listen in a very literal way. Adolescents begin to make deeper connections. Adults notice conceptual meanings and are able to integrate the teachings into the breadth of their experience. This is the brilliance of our traditions—our stories are seeds, encoding multiple meanings that grow and change with the passage of time. They are a dynamic, engaging conversation that requires personal engagement and refection and that our people embody and carry with them throughout their lives. They are meant to provide comfort, meaning, and a sense of belonging within our families and communities.

As Nishnaabeg, we are taught to see ourselves as part of these narratives, and it is the responsibility of each generation to tell these stories in a way that is relevant and meaningful to the way we live. It is my hope that *The Gift Is in the Making* resonates with our current lives and experience while celebrating diversity, gentleness, and humour, and that it encourages interconnection and interdependence among us. My aim in presenting the versions of these ancient narratives in *The Gift Is in the Making* is to liberate a few of them from the colonial contexts in which they are too often documented—in which we see the marginalization and subjugation of female characters and spirits, a focus on hierarchy and authoritarian power, and an overly moral and judgmental tone, for example.

The way I have chosen to retell these stories—that is, in the context of Nishnaabeg storytelling traditions—means that I use repetition, abstraction, metaphor, and multi-dimensionality to communicate meaning. I encourage all readers of this collection to seek and cherish the diversity of understandings and interpretations of these stories and to find their own personal meanings within them. These are the gentlest of stories, told in the kindest of ways, and I have chosen them for their simple narrative arcs, but readers should not assume that all Nishnaabeg stories are like this; we have stories that are extremely complex and that go into very challenging places. The body of Nishnaabeg oral literature is vast and dynamic, and *The Gift Is in the Making* opens just a very small window into our oral literature. It is but one link in a long chain of oral and written work, work that is collectively owned by the Nishnaabeg. To acknowledge this, a portion of the royalties from *The Gift Is in the Making* will be donated to Nishnaabemowin regeneration projects.

STORYTELLING TRADITIONS AMONGST THE NISHNAABEG

There are many different storytelling traditions amongst the Nishnaabeg, and there are many different ways to interpret them. I have been taught that certain stories, the Aadsookaanag (Aadizookaanag), sacred stories, are to be told only during the winter months. There are many reasons for this tradition, some practical and some spiritual. Wintertime in Nishnaabeg territory is cold, dark, and long. In the past, storytelling was a wonderful way of keeping spirits up during times of hardship. And limiting the telling of the Aadsookaanag to the wintertime also challenged storytellers to stretch and expand during the spring, summer, and fall, when storytellers told the Dbaajimowinan, personal narratives, histories, experiences, and stories about animals. This is what keeps our personal and family histories and narratives alive.

The interpretation of these traditions varies from community to community and from individual to individual. Some storytellers tell stories when opportunities arise regardless of the season; others hold a certain set of stories for telling only once the snow is on the ground or when certain constellations appear in the November sky; and still others engage in ceremony when they deviate from certain restrictions.

There are many good reasons to carry these traditions forward. In my own practice, I look forward to telling certain stories in the wintertime when my family is sometimes stuck inside for long periods of time, although within the context of my own family, I have made exceptions. I've learned to seek out other kinds of stories to tell in the other parts of the year. In the part of Nishnaabeg territory I come from, the Elders caution against telling Nanabush (also known as Nanabozhoo or Wenabozhoo) stories outside of winter, or some even saying the name "Nana-bush" outside of winter, and I continue to honour their teachings in my oral practice. I want to be careful that I always tell these stories in a good way. The wintertime is a good time to do this because the spirits are farther away from the earth and there is less chance of embarrassing any of beings that guide me through my life. I encourage readers to respect the different interpretations of these traditions and to find out the storytelling traditions in their territory. Developing respectful relationships with Elders and storytellers directly is the best way to honour these traditions.

Finally, when writing this, I always imagined my audience to be Nishnaabeg kids because they are both the inspiration and motivation for this project. I also see ways non-Nishnaabeg children can draw important messages and thoughts from these stories too. For other, older Nishnaabeg readers, I hope they enjoy these stories and seek out opportunities to hear other versions orally and in Nishnaabemowin so that we may collectively regenerate our relationship to the land, our oral traditions and our language. I also encourage non-Native readers to seek out the histories and perspectives of the Indigenous Peoples' territory they call home and work towards becoming a decolonizing influence where they live.

A Note on Gender

Gzhwe Mnidoo—the great unknown, the Creator, life force, essence, the one who loves us completely and unconditionally—has no gender association within Nishnaabemowin. Too often, in English the gender of Gzhwe Mnidoo is assumed and written to be male. In keeping with Nishnaabemowin and the teachings I carry, I have not assigned a male gender to Gzhwe Mnidoo in this collection.

Similarly, Tomson Highway writes in the introduction of *Kiss of the Fur Queen* (Toronto: Anchor Canada, 1995) that Nanabush within the Cree and Ojibwe languages also does not have a gender association. He writes, "[Nanabush] is theoretically neither exclusively male nor exclusively female, or is both simultaneously" (p. i). Some people know Nanabush to be a male spirit. Others believe Nanabush travels freely among all genders. I think everyone can agree that, as a master transformer, Nanabush can and does appear in a variety of different forms in our stories— forms representing all kinds of humans, animals, plants, and even elements. This becomes one of the problems with telling the stories in English where there are (only) two gendered pronouns, *him* and *her*—an issue that simply does not exist when these stories are told within Nishnaabemowin. In order to emphasize this transformative quality of Nanabush, I use both *he/him* and *she/her.* The Nanabush inside of me believes it is important to play with colonial gender, sexuality, and racial constructions, and I think it is important to re-imagine Nanabush in all of these beautiful forms and not just the young, able-bodied male so often presented to us.

A NOTE ON LANGUAGE

This book is sprinkled with Nishnaabemowin so that children and very new language learners will begin to recognize our words. It is meant only to spark an interest in our language, not to teach the language. It is my hope that, when readers become more proficient in Nishnaabemowin, they will move onto stories told in the language by The Ojibwe Cultural Foundation, Anton Treuer or Basil Johnston (see the Further Reading section at the end of this book). In Mississauga, or Michi Saagiig Nishnaabeg territory, our way of speaking drops some of the syllables our northern and western relatives pronounce. I love this diversity. I've written the words how I hear them in the place where I live. I have used the Fiero system of writing.

This collection is a retelling of previously published, traditional Nishnaabeg stories with the exception of "Good Neighbours," which I wrote to teach my own children about resistance and the importance of standing up for the land.

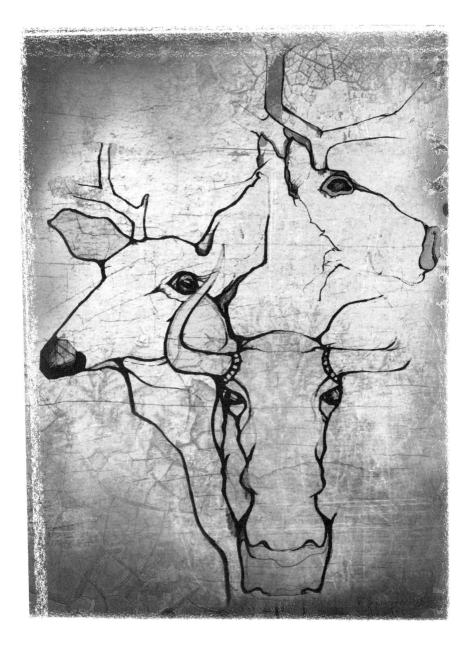

1

Our Treaty with the Hoof Nation

In a time long ago, all the Waawaashkeshiwag, Moozoog, and Adikwag, the deer, moose, and caribou, suddenly disappeared from Kina Gchi Nishnaabeg-ogaming.

Well, maybe it wasn't so suddenly. At first, nobody noticed. The relatives of the Hoof Clan had to be very patient. But, after a while, people were starting to notice some changes.

In fall, dagwaagin, hunters, came back with no meat.

When snow blanketed the earth, the people didn't even see a single track in the snow—for the whole bboon!

By ziigwan, the people were getting worried. No one had seen a deer for nearly a year. No one had seen a moose for nearly a year, and no one could even remember the last time they saw a caribou.

The people got worried. Were the Waawaashkeshiwag lost? Were the Moozoog sick and unable to get out of bed? Had the Adikwag been kidnapped by aliens? Is this all a game of hide-and-go-seek gone wrong?

The Nishnaabeg wished they had been paying better attention. They wished they had been taking better care of their relatives.

The people started feeling sad and guilty and worried—and hungry. And do you know what happens when you're feeling sad and guilty and worried and hungry? That sad and guilty and

worried and hungry mixes altogether and stews and grows and
Grows
AND GRows
AND GROws
AND GROWs.

And then that sad and guilty and worried and hungry turns
into something different.

Those Amikwag get a little slappy with their tails.

The Jijaakwag start to get a little bossy.

The Migiziwag start to get nippy.

Those Makwag get even more growly than usual.

Those Zhigaagwag get a little careless with their medicine,
spraying it all over.

And then everything starts to go in the wrong direction.

So, those Nishinaabeg decided to do something before everything got all lost. They got up before the sun one morning, lit a
sacred fire. They prayed, sang, and offered their semaa.

After a long discussion, where everyone spoke what was in
their hearts, the people decided to send their fastest runners out
in the four directions to find those hoofed ones.

Those runners ran for four days. Ziigwan was the first to come
back. She hadn't seen so much as a tuft of hair. Then Niibin arrived,
exhausted, and reported the same. When Dagwaagin came back, he
reported that he'd seen no evidence of deer, moose, or caribou either.

Finally, Bboon returned. He was exhausted and said, "When
I was in the very north part of our land, I saw one young deer.
She explained to me that her relatives had left our territory for-
ever because they felt disrespected."

The Nishnaabeg were silent. They felt sad and lost. They
thought about how they had been wasting the meat of the Hoof
Clan. They thought about how they hadn't been sharing with
all their community members. They thought about how they'd
killed deer even when they didn't need them.

The people didn't know what to do, so they decided to go and meet with the oldest and wisest people they knew. Those Elders decided to send a delegation of diplomats, spiritual people, and mediators to go and visit the Hoof Clan.

After some negotiation, the people learned that the Hoof Clan had left their territory because the Nishnaabeg were no longer honouring them. They had been wasting their meat and not treating their bodies with the proper reverence. The Hoof Clan had withdrawn from the territory and their relationship with the Nishnaabeg. They had stopped participating.

The diplomats, spiritual people, and mediators just listened. They listened to all the stories and teachings the Hoof Clan had to share. They spent several long days of listening, of acknowledging, of discussing, and of negotiating. All the parties thought about what they could give up to restore the relationship. Finally, the Hoof Clan and the Nishnaabeg agreed to honour and respect the lives and beings of the Hoof Clan, in life and in death. They assured the Hoof Clan that they would use the flesh of the Waawaashkeshiwag, Moozoog, and Adikwag wisely and that they would look after and protect deer, moose, and caribou habitat and homes. They told the Hoof Clan that they would share their meat with all in need, take only what they needed, and use everything they took, and they would rely on other food sources when times were tough for the Hoof Clan. The Nishnaabeg promised to leave semaa to acknowledge the anguish they have brought upon the animals for killing one of their members so that they might live, and they told the Hoof Clan they would perform special ceremonies and rituals whenever they took an animal.

In exchange, the Hoofed Animals would return to our territory so that Nishnaabeg people could feed themselves and their families. They agreed to give up their lives whenever the Nishnaabeg were in need.

So the Waawaashkeshiwag, Moozoog, and Adikwag returned to the land of the Nishnaabeg. To this day, we still go through the many rituals outlined that day when we kill a member of the Hoof Clan. We remember those original Hoof Clan teachings about how to share land without interfering with other nations. We remember how to take care of the land so we can all bring forth more lives. We honour our treaty relationship with Waawaashkeshiwag, Woozoog, and Adikwag—so we can all live good lives.

Nishnaabemowin: Waawaashkesh is deer; mooz is moose; adik is caribou; Gchi Nishnaabeg-ogaming is "the place we all live and work together" according to Elder Doug Williams from Curve Lake First Nation; dawaagin is fall; bboon is winter; amikwag is beavers; moozoog are moose plural; makwag are bears; jijaakwag (ajijaakwag) are cranes; migizig are bald eagles; zhigaagwag are skunks; semaa (asemaa) is tobacco; and ziigwan is the early part of spring when the snow is melting, the ice is breaking up and the sap is flowing; niibin is summer; waawaashkeshiwag are deer (plural), adikwag are caribou (plural).

2

THE BAAGAATAA'AWA GAME THAT CHANGED EVERYTHING

Usually, things are quiet in bboon. Mama is all rolled up warm in her white blanket in a deep rest after all that creating and then all that celebrating. Shhhhhhhh.

It's time for renewal. Makwa is dreaming, others are visiting Zhaawanong. The forest has a quiet, nearly empty feel to it.

Usually.

This year there was a kerfuffle. Instead of all quiet, it was all chirpy. Instead of snowflakes softly falling, feathers were flying like mini-tornadoes. Instead of helping, there was only snip-snapping.

Those Bineshiinyag were hungry, because they couldn't find enough to eat.

"Nbakade! Nbakade!" they sang.

"Nbakade! Nbakade!" they chirped.

"Nbakade! Nbakade!" they cawed.

"Nbakade! Nbakade!" they cried.

And then they started to argue.

"That's my seed."

"Those are MYYYY dinner."

"GET YOUR OWN LUNCH!"

And then, that big fight got bigger and bigger. Until all the Bineshiinyag were arguing and fighting and being very big meanies. It was like a fire, and everyone was throwing more and more wood onto that fire and it was getting bigger and bigger. And then—it spread to the animals.

Amik started getting overly chewy.

Makwa started to be extra growly, even in her sleep!

Nika got a little too pokey with her beak.

Giigoonh…oh, that Giigoonh was just slippery, sliding out of all kinds of deals and promises.

Maybe that Gidigaa Bizhiw's claws get out and don't go back in, and pretty soon, everyone is all snip-snappy-yelly, and fur is flying everywhere.

Pretty soon, the Nishnaabeg notice, but not the big ones, not this time, not yet. Nope, those big ones don't notice when things go off balance at the beginning. They always notice too late. It was those little ones that noticed. Those little ones are always paying attention. They notice. Kids notice.

Those kids noticed, and they did the right thing. They told that old Nokomis, and that old Nokomis knew just what to do.

That old Nokomis says we're gonna have a meeting at noon at the big cedar tree. And so Pichi puts up a Facebook group and invites everyone, and everyone confirms they are coming, and then no one shows up at noon at the Chi'giizhikatig.

So, the next day, that old Nokomis says we're gonna have another meeting. This time a Talking Circle, and this time Pichi goes from house to house and tells everyone to meet at Chi'giizhikatig. This time everyone comes, and it starts out going good. Then Giigohn starts talking, well, maybe kinda complaining, and maybe kind of going on and on and on and on, and, Bear, she get all mad and start yelling from the other side of the circle and soon fur is flying, and nobody listening, and Nokomis just leaves.

The next day, that old Nokomis tries ceremony. She gets everyone all lined up by the Chi-gizhiikatig, but, just as she's lighting the smudge, Nika says it's her turn to be shkabewis, but Amik and Gidigaa Bizhiw also think it's their turn, and pretty soon fur is flying and nobody is listening, and Nokomis lights the smudge by herself, but no one is even left for the ceremony.

The fourth day, Nokomis decides everybody needs to run off some steam. "Everybody meet me at noon at the big gizhiikatig," she say, "because it's gonna be all fun and games, and there is a prize."

Well, everyone likes a prize, so everyone shows up.

That old lady split the group into two teams. Animals on one side. Birds on the other.

Only Pakwaanaajiinh is left standing by the gizhiikatig.

Nokomis tell the birds, Bat is on their team.

"Bat can't be on our team because she has fur," Bineshiinyag say.

Nokomis tell the animals the bat is on their team.

"Bat can't be on our team because Bat has wings," Animals say.

Nokomis tell the birds the bat is on their team.

The birds say, "That bat is too tiny and way too tired, and she has that baby bat that is always screaming, and she has to spend ALL of her time nursing that little guy just to keep him quiet."

Nokomis takes a deep breath.

Fur just about to fly again, when Waawaashkesh gets the animals together. She tells them that Bat might just be useful, because she can echolocate things in the dark and because she can fly, and, plus, they don't have to put her on the field, she can just sit on the bench.

So the animals agree. Even Makwa. The game starts.

Bat hangs upside down under the tree by the bench nursing her little batling.

The first day the game doesn't go so well. A little too rough. Nokomis gets tired blowing her whistle all the time, and there is so much pushing and shoving that no one even hears her whistle. Also, no one even gets close to the net—0-0.

The second day goes better, only a few scuffles in front of the net—0-0.

The third day, everyone getting a little tired. Still 0-0.

People starting to loose interest a bit. Amik start sneaking off to her lodge when no one looking.

The fourth day, everyone starts wondering why they're play-ing. Everyone so tired they forget what the fight is about. By sundown, it is looking like the game might never end. All this time, Bat been nursing her baby, hanging under that tree. And on that fourth day at sundown, out of the corner of her eye, she sees something coming towards her.

You know how mamas have super-powerful peripheral vision? You know how mamas have super-fast reaction times? Well, that bat just kept nursing her baby with one wing. With the other, she stretched out way below her head and caught that ball.

And then she tucked that nursing baby under her wing and held onto that stick and flew like the wind to right in front of the birds' net, and she fired that ball right between the goalposts.

And the crowd erupted with cheers. And the animals came running to congratulate her, and that baby bat just kept right on nursing away. And those Bineshiinyag come and congratulate her too, because they so happy that the game is finally over.

Then Bineshiinyag go and have a big meeting with Nokomis at the chi-gizhiikatig. They meet with Nokomis because it had become their responsibility to solve the food shortage, a very big responsibility.

By the light of that big Nokomis-Giizis, the Bineshiinyag decide that those that can fly to visit their friends in the Zhaawa-nong will do so every dagwaagin. In the spring they will return to Kina Gchi Nishnaabeg-ogaming, and it has been that way ever since. They're excited for their adventure. The ones that will stay are happy too, because they will have enough food. Everybody is happy.

Even Nokomis.

Actually, especially Nokomis, because all her children are happy and healthy—and nothing is better than that.

Nishnaabemowin: Bagaataa'awe refers to the action of passing a ball back and forth and is the Nishnaabe name for lacrosse; bboon is winter; makwa is bear; zhaawanong is south; bineshiinyag are birds; nbakade means I'm hungry; amik means beaver; nika means goose; gidigaa bizhiw means spotted lynx or bobcat; giigonh is fish, pichi (opichi) is a robin; Nokomis is Grandmother; chi'giizhikatig is big cedar tree; shkabewis (oshkabewis) is a helper in a ceremony; pakwaanaajiinh (apakwaanaajiinh) is a bat; waawaashkesh (waawaashkeshi) is a deer; Nokomis Giizis is the moon; dawaagin is the fall; and Kina Gchi Nishnaabeg-ogaming means the "big place where we all live and work together" or Nishnaabeg territory, according to Curve Lake Elder Doug Williams.

3

ALL OUR RELATIONS

The old people say that we are all related—not just to the people that live in our house, but to the plants, the animals, the air, the water, and the land.

Our Nokomis is the moon. The earth is our first mama. Our father is the sky. Our Mishomis is the sun.

We are just one big, beautiful family, with many different branches.

The Nishnaabeg have always known this. Because of this knowledge, we have lived a fantastic, marvellous life here on Chi'Mikinakong for a cabillion generations.

But, sometimes, just sometimes, we get busy. We forget the small things, and, when we do, we learn that they are actually big, important things.

This is exactly what happened a long, long time ago.

Our ancestors were very smart people, and they knew more than anybody about how to live in our territory in a good way because they paid attention to the Elders and to the animals and to the plants. They paid attention to each other.

Usually, things were very good in the Niibin, but one summer, the Nishnaabeg were finding it very hard to find food. The ode'minan had bloomed, but there were no berries. It was the same with the miskominag and the miinan. Many of the flowers were missing, and many of the insects, too. The hunters had caught a bear to eat, but the meat was very sour. The people were worried.

They called all the Elders, the Grandmothers, the Grandfathers and the Medicine People together and asked for advice. After a ceremony and a meeting, the Elders and the Grandmothers and the Grandfathers and the Medicine People suggested that the people go and ask Makwa.

So they went and talked with Makwa.

Makwa said, "Don't ask me. Ask Aamoo."

So the people went and visited Aamoo.

Aamoo said, "Don't ask me. Ask Waawaasgonenh."

So the people went and visited with Waawaasgoneh, and Waawaasgoneh told them a very sad story about the rose, Ginii.

"A long time ago, there were lots and lots of flowers," Waawaasgoneh began. "There were lots and lots of roses. All summer long, they bloomed and smiled and waited for the Nishnaabeg to notice. But no one ever did. Not until the fall, when it was time to pick the rose hips so the Nishnaabeg would have vitamin C all winter long. The roses felt lonely, unappreciated, and taken for granted. They felt miserable and used. So the roses, they left."

The Nishnaabeg realized what they had done.

Waawaasgoneh continued: "Then Aamoo couldn't find any nectar to make honey, and then Makwa couldn't find any honey to help her get through the long winter, and now you, the Nishnaabeg, are very hungry."

The Nishnaabeg listened and thought about this problem. They asked those Old People what to do. The Elders, the Grandmothers, the Grandfathers and the Medicine People had a big, long, kinda-boring-for-the-kids meeting. At the end, they all agreed. They told the people to go and see the Bineshiinyag. They told the people to ask Bineshiinyag to fly all around and find a Ginii and bring it back.

So the Nishnaabeg went to talk to the birds, and those birds agreed to help. They got up very early in the morning and went out in every direction, searching for Ginii. They searched for long hours, day after day, in the north, the south, the east, and the west. But, day after day, they returned with empty beaks.

"There are none left," reported Migizi.

No sooner had the bald eagle spoken than little Naanooshkeshiinh, the ruby-throated hummingbird, flew up with a wilted rose plant in her mouth.

"Naanooshkeshiinh! Naanooshkeshiinh!" the people said softly.

The Nishnaabeg gently took the plant and put Ginii's roots in soil. They were so worried because Ginii just lay there on the soil, tired and sad.

They sang to her.

They gave her nibiish.

They made sure her leaves felt the morning sun. Most importantly, and in their quietest and most gentle voices, they talked to her. They told her how much they had missed her, how much they loved her.

They talked about the deep raspberry colour of her petals. They talked about how soft those petals were on their cheeks. They talked about the tea they loved to make out of her rose hips.

After a few days, Ginii began to get stronger, and, in a few more days, she stood up. When she was strong, the Nishnaabeg used her roots to plant more flowers. Soon, those flowers spread to more parts of the bush.

Then the Nishnaabeg found the Aamoog and showed them where all the new plants were. Those Aamoog got busy pollinating. Soon there were lots of roses, lots of fat Aamoog, and there was lots of sweet, sweet honey.

This made Makwa very happy, because he was also getting fat from eating all of that good honey.

And, soon, the Nishnaabeg were feeling much stronger and much healthier, too, because they ate that good, sweet, bear meat. After that, the Nishnaabeg remembered Ginii and all the flowers in their land.

So, you see how important each one of those plants and animals are? We should never destroy anything.

That's what those old Elders always say.

Nishnaabemowin: Nokomis is Grandmother; Mishomis is Grandfather; Chi'Mikinakong is the big place of the turtle, or turtle island and is a Mississauga name for North America according to Curve Lake Elder Doug Williams; niibin is summer; ode'minan (ode'iminan) are strawberries; miskominag are raspberries; and miinan are blueberries; makwa means bear; aamoo is a bee; aamoog are bees; waawaasgonenh is a flower; ginii (oginii-waabigwan) is a rose; bineshiinyag are birds; migizi is a bald eagle; naanooshkeshiinh is a ruby-throated humming bird; and nibiish is water.

4

A GIFT FROM A VERY SMART LITTLE GREEN FROG

One day, Kwezens was out with Kokum picking berries, when they came across Ginebig looking for her lunch.

Ginebig was slithering around on the ground, moving in and out of the berry bushes, when she came across a little green zhaawshko-magkiins.

"Watch," said Kokum.

Kwezens watched, feeling nervous and scared for that cutey—little green omakakii. Ginebig was moving fast, dreaming of that tasty zhaawshko-magkiins in her mouth. But that little zhaawshko-magkiins wasn't just cute—he was also very smart, and he hopped right into a patch of Niimkiibag.

Ginebig stopped dead in her tracks.

Zhaawshko-magkiins waited.

Ginebig's mom had told her to never, ever go into a patch of Niimkiibag; otherwise she'd feel the itchy burning pain of thunderbolts all over her skin for days. So Ginebig knew she'd just have to wait.

Ginebig waited and waited and waited and waited, and then she was so bored from all that waiting that she felt like she was going to explode if she waited even one more second.

Finally, she gave up and slithered away, dreaming of a different kind of lunch.

When Zhaawshko-magkiins was sure that Ginebig was gone, Zhaawshko-magkiins hopped out of the Niimkiibag and directly into a patch of Majimashkikinaandawi'on, jewelweed, which usually grows right beside the poison ivy. He chewed off a stem and then lathered his whole body in that good medicine.

"Nahow," said Kokum, "if you should ever find yourself in the same situation as Zhaawshko-magkiins, covered in Niimki-ibag, you'll know just what to do".

And that is how our Medicine People learned the antidote to Niimkiibag.

Nishnaabemowin: Kwezens (ikwezens) is a girl; Kokum is Grandma; Ginebig is snake; zhaawshko-magkiins is a small green frog (Curve Lake); omakakii is frog; Niimkiibag is literally "thunder plant" or poison ivy; majimashkikinaandawi'on is jewelweed; and nahow is okay.

5

She Knew Exactly What To Do

It was deep in the bboon.
The days were short and cold
and everyone was sick.
Their wiigwaaman were full of
blowing and coughing and fever
first it was Binoojiins
then Mishomis
then Nokomis
then Binoojiinh
then Noos, and
then finally, it was Doodoom.

Soon, the mashkiki had run
right
out.
They were so sick that they had run
right
out
of mashkiki.

Nokomis sent the runner out to the next
village to get some more from their
Mashkikiiwininiikwe. But the runner took sick
and collapsed before reaching the lake.

Nooshenh knew what she had to do.
She was the only one healthy.
With all the coughing and sneezing and blowing,
it wouldn't be long before she was sick too.
So she packed up some food, her flint and
all the brave she could fit into her heart
and she set out to the next village.

It was very windy.
It was very, very cold.
She walked through the sugar bush,
past the place where they picked wild leeks,
past where the fiddleheads grow,
beside the berry patches
and the Labrador tea, until she got to zaaga'igan.

The ice was thick on the lake
and noodin was fierce and whippy.
But she kept walking.

Finally, when she was just about to the other side
that old Mashkikiiwininiikwe saw her.
And so that old Mashkikiiwininiikwe got her
shkode going big.
She got her niibiishaboo on the fire.
She got ready.
She knew that, when Nooshenh got there, she'd
be cold, tired, and hungry.

Then that old Medicine Woman went and picked her up
and brought her home
wrapped her in warm wabooz blankets
gave her tea and soup
and told her to rest.
"Waabang, we will go together and take the mashkiki to your
family."

It was a good idea, but Nooshenh woke up
in the middle of the night
sick with worry, whispered miigwech
and slipped out of that old lady's lodge.

The ice was thick on the lake
and noodin was fierce and whippy.
Nooshenh kept walking. Across zaaga'igan,
past the Labrador tea,
beside the berry patches,
past where the fiddleheads grow,
past the wild leeks,
through the sugar bush.
It was very, very cold.
It was very blowy.

Finally, she could see the smoke from her family's lodges. By now,
the sun was high in the noonday sky.
The snow was warming up and so, of course,
one step in that deep snow and she was sunk.

She struggled.
She lost her makizinan.
She lost her patience.
But she didn't lose her fight.

On she went, barefoot, all the way home to her lodge.
Her family was very happy to see her.
They listened to her story.
They drank that mashkiki
and wrapped her feet in medicine
and warm blankets.

And the next summer in the exact spot where she lost her
makizinan

grew the most beautiful pink flowers
anyone had ever seen.
Nokomis called them
Makizinkwe, woman's shoe,
in honour of her brave Nooshehn.
She knew exactly what to do.

Nishnaabemowin: Makizinikwe is one of our names for lady's slipper; bboon is winter; wiigwaaman are homes or lodges; binoojiyens (abinoojiyens) is baby; Mishomis is Grandfather; Nokomis is Grandmother; binoojiinh (abinoojiinh) is a child; noos is Father; doodoom is Mama (an older name that a child would call a mother—literally my breastfeeder); mashkiki is medicine; Mashkikiiwininiikwe is Medicine Woman; noozhenh means grandchild; zaaga'igan is lake; noodin is the wind; shkode is a fire; niibiishaboo (aniibiishaaboo) is tea; wabooz is rabbit; waabang is tomorrow; and miigwech means thank you.

6

Zhingwaak Gets a Little Snippy

Mewnzha, mewnzha, mewnzha, Wiigwaasaatig was marching around the forest bragging.

"I really am so beautiful. I love my skin. It is perfect. I have the perfect skin, I do not even need to moisturize, not even one little bit."

Mostly, all the other mitigoog ignored Wiigwaasaatig, but the bragging continued. "I really am the most useful tree in the forest, as well. The Nishnaabeg can use me to make houses, containers, canoes, and abstract art. Really, I think the forest only needs one tree and that tree is me."

Giizhikatig, who was also a great friend of the Nishnaabeg, was silent, thinking that Giizhikatig, the cedar or the sky tree, also gave the people food, medicine, and shelter.

Ninatigoog, who had just finished sharing his sap with the Nishnaabeg, was also quiet.

Zhingwaak, the pine, the tree that teaches about peace, was also silent, but Wiigwaasaatig didn't even notice.

"I'm just going to sway and dance a little so you all can bask in my beauty," Wiigwaasaatig sang out.

Zhingwaak was still silent, but Zhingwaak was feeling irritated.

"I'm just going to sing a bit as well, because my voice is very sweet, and I'm sure you'll enjoy me. I am so enjoyable."

Zhingwaak's body started to sway a bit with all this mad building up.

"Great idea, Zhingwaak! That little breeze you are making rattles my leaves, and it makes me look and sound even better," said Wiigwaasi-mitig.

This made Zhingwaak's body sway a little bit more and a little bit more, until the little breeze turned into chi'noodin.

"Whoaa, Ziingwaak! You're getting a little crazy. Your needles are starting to touch my beautiful bark. Settle down, Ziingwaak! We wouldn't want to mark my bark. It's so perfect the way it is," said Wiigwaasaatig.

But it was too late. The big wind of Zhingwaak had already left needle marks all over Wiigwaasaatig's skin.

Zhingwaak eventually calmed down and got all her anger back under control.

Wiigwaasaatig calmed down too, even though he had needle marks all over his skin.

After some time, Wiigwaasaatig stopped bragging so much and started to see all the gifts the other trees gave as well. Eventually, he found that being a good relative filled his heart much fuller than bragging about how great he was. He grew to love his body the way it was, pine needles and all.

Nishnaabemowin: Mewnzha means a long time ago; Nigitchi Nendas means "I have a big head" or "I'm arrogant"; mitigoog are trees; wiigwaasaatig (wiigwaasi-mitig) is a birch tree; gizhiikatig is a cedar tree; ninaatig is a maple tree; and zhingwaak is a white pine; chi noodin means it is very windy.

7

Please Be Careful When You're Getting Smart

A lot of people come to university to get smart. Education is the new buffalo. But, I say that it is important to stay smart while you are getting smart, and I learned that one from old Nanabush.

This story takes place a long, long, long time ago. Mewnzha, mewnzha, mewnzha.

It was summertime, and Nanabush was in the forest, feeling pretty hungry but also kind of lazy. He got to thinking that all his problems could be solved if only he were smarter.

"Owah," said Nanabush. "If I were only smarter, I wouldn't have to spend all this time hunting. I bet those animals would come right to my lodge."

"Owah," said Nanabush. "If I were only smarter, I wouldn't have to spend all this time fishing. I bet those fish would jump right into my jiimaan."

"Owah," said Nanabush. "If I were only smarter, I wouldn't have to spend all this time gathering and preparing medicines. I bet those medicines would jump right into my bag all ready to go if I got sick."

"This would be a good life, if I were smart."

So Nanabush thought about how he could get smart, and, when he couldn't come up with any ideas, he went to see old Nokomis.

"Nokomis, I think my life would be so easy and so much better if I were smarter," said Nanabush.

"Ehn, you're right. Smart people do have a good life. It's true," replied Nokomis.

"Do you know how I could get smart, Nokomis? Because if I were smarter, everything would be a lot less work. I wouldn't have to spend all this time hunting. I bet those animals would come right to my lodge. I wouldn't have to spend all this time fishing. I bet those fish would jump right into my jiimaan. I wouldn't have to spend all this time gathering and preparing medicines. I bet those medicines would jump right into my bag all ready to go if I got sick."

"Hmmm," said Nokomis. "I do know this place in the forest, and in this special place is a bush, and on that bush are some very special berries, smart berries. One handful, and you start to get smarter, immediately."

"Oh, Nokomis," said Nanabush. "This is exactly what I need. Take me, take me, take me, TAAAKE MEEEEEE!"

"Nahow," said Nokomis. "I will take you, but you have to calm down. It's a long walk."

"I AM calm, and I'm very good at long walks. Ambe Maajaadaa!"

And so Nanabush and Nokomis began to walk down the path to find the smart berries. They walked and walked, and finally they came to a plant with tiny red berries on it.

"Are these the berries? Are these the smart berries, Nokomis? Are they? Are they? Are they?"

"Gaawiin, those are ode'minan, heart berries. Those aren't the smart berries."

A little while later, they came across another kind of red berry.

"Are these the berries? Are these the smart berries, Nokomis? Are they? Are they? Are they?"

"Gaawiin, those are miskominag, blood berries. Those aren't the smart berries."

A little while later, they came across another kind of berry, a blueberry.

"Are these the berries? Are these the smart berries, Nokomis? Are they? Are they? Are they?"

"Gaawiin, those are miinan, blueberries. Those aren't the smart berries."

They walked some more. Nanabush was getting tired, but he wasn't complaining. He wanted those smart berries badly.

Finally, Nokomis stopped walking. "We're here," she announced.

Nanabush looked around for the big, delicious berries.

"Where are they, Nokomis?"

"They are here, Nanabush, on the ground."

"Those don't look like berries."

"These are the smart berries."

"Those don't smell like berries."

"These are the smart berries. One handful and you'll start getting smarter almost immediately."

"Nahow," said Nanabush, taking a big handful and putting them into his mouth. AAAAAAHHHHHHHH, BLECK, YUCK! These aren't berries, Nokomis! These are waawaashkesh, poop!"

"See, Nanabush, you are getting smarter already."

Nishnaabemowin: Mewnzha is long ago, and is an old way of starting traditional stories that gives some indication of time, depending upon how many are used, Doug Williams, Elder, Curve Lake First Nation; jiimaan is Canoe; Nokomis is Grandmother; ehn means yes; nahow is okay; ambe maajaadaa means let's go; ode'minan are strawberries; gaawiin means no; miskominag are raspberries; miinan are blueberries; waawaashkesh (waawaashkeshi) is a deer.

8

IT'S YOU WHO MAKES THE NAME POWERFUL

Have you ever felt jealous?

Well, one day Nanabush was feeling jealous. He thought all the other animals in the forest had better, more powerful names than he did. He wanted a new, better, more powerful name. Something like Eagle Thunderbolt Man or maybe Hunts Way Better Than Everyone Else.

"Ehn," thought Nanabush. "I need a new name."

So Nanabush got all the other animals in the forest together to convince them that they all needed new names.

"Our names are old and boring," Nanabush lectured. "We need new ones, ones that more accurately reflect the great beings we've become."

The animals agreed. So, they took some semaa to ask Nokomis. Nokomis agreed and set the Naming Ceremony for the next morning at sunrise.

Nanabush was so excited, he could not contain himself. He went zooming around the forest. Then, he went zooming around the lake. Then, he zoomed up to the top of the highest hill.

Finally, the other animals were getting sleepy and going to bed, but Nanabush didn't think this was necessarily a good idea.

"If I stay up all night, I'll be the first one at the ceremony tomorrow," he said to himself. "That way, I'll get the very best name."

He did jumping jacks to stay awake. Then, he ate all his food cache. Then, he drank all the tea he had. Then, he told himself all the jokes he knew. Finally, by about 4:30 AM, he fell fast asleep.

He slept and slept and slept and slept, until naakwe, noon. He woke with a start. "WHAT TIME IS IT?" he roared, noticing the sun already high in the sky. "GAAWIIN, I'm late!" He ran to the ceremony without changing out of his pajamas and brushing his teeth. He got there just as Nokomis was handing out the last name.

"Don't worry," said Nokomis, in a very reassuring voice. "I have the perfect name left for you."

Nokomis stood in the centre of the circle, hanging onto Nanbush's hand, ready to announce his new name to the four directions. She turned to the east.

"Bozhoo, Nanabush."

Nokomis announced his name to the three remaining directions, but Nanabush couldn't hear her because he was so upset. He threw himself on the ground. He screeched and cried. He pounded his fists on the ground and kicked the air.

Nokomis watched the meltdown, and, when Nanabush started to wear himself out, she asked, "Nanabush, what is wrong?"

Nanabush explained that he wanted a powerful name like Sparkly White Bear or Super Duper Strong Medicine Moose Man. "Hmmm," thought Nokomis. "Hmmmm."

After thinking for a bit, Nokomis said, "Nanabush, you've got it backwards. It's not the name that makes you powerful, its *you* who makes the name powerful." Then she gave Nanabush an enormous hug.

"Holy," said Nanabush. "You're right, I've got it all backwards!"

So, after that, Nanabush set out to make his name powerful by helping, sharing, teaching, singing, dancing, and loving.

Nishnaabemowin: Ehn means yes; Nokomis is Grandmother; semaa (asemaa) is tobacco; gaawiin means no; naakwe is noon.

9

GOOD NEIGHBOURS

The Nimkiig Binesiwag live up high on a mountain in a very big nest, so they can watch over everything. The Nishnaabeg almost never see them. But, in the spring and summer, you can hear them when they fly over. Those old ones put out some semaa when the thunderbirds are coming because they know the Niimkiig Binesiwag protect us and keep us safe—even though their big boomy sounds are kind of scary. Those old ones know the Niimkiig Binesiwag bring with them the rain that cleanses the land and feeds those thirsty plants.

Nahow, when this story happens, things are not so good for those Nishnaabeg. Things are not so good.

Most people had enough food, so that wasn't it. Not this time.

Most people had houses, so that wasn't it. Not this time.

Most people were practising their ways, so that wasn't it. Not this time.

This time, the problem was with the neighbours—those ones who moved in beside the Nishnaabeg. They were partying all the time. Loud. All the time. Never taking care. Tramping all over those plants Nishnaabeg use to heal. Eating everything out of the Nishnaabeg's garden. Building a big wooden deck fence all around the Nishnaabeg's house, so nobody can get in and out any more. Cutting down trees for *no reason*. Peeing in the water.

That's right. Peeing in the water. I KNOW. Can you imagine? What kind of people pee in the water?

But it was more than just pee. They would cut down all kinds of trees, put them into special machines, and out comes birchbark. Long, beautiful sheets of birchbark. But they don't make any canoes. No, siree. They drew lines on sheets and then they threw them away. That's what they did with most of the stuff they made. They threw it away.

That machine, it's not so special after all. It's not so magic. While it makes all this beautiful birchbark for no reason, it also makes this really-bad-medicine-soup that make everybody sick—even those animals and the fish. Everybody. It was a slow kind of sickness, that one, the kind that sneaks up on you. Those neighbours had no place to put that really-bad-medicine-soup. So they built this big pot at the base of the mountain, and they put it in there. They thought they'd keep it there until they could think of what to do with it.

But, after a lot of years, that big pot of really-bad-medicine-soup is still there. It's starting to go funny colours. Leaking out. That one that lives underwater and protects the lake says she can see it leaking. Funny colour of blue, it leaks. The big pot of really-bad-medicine-soup is so big the Nimkiig Binesiwag can see it from space.

And these Nishnaabeg, they tried everything. They had their neighbours over for dessert, to try and be friends. Rhubarb pie. That's what they all had. Homemade. Good stuff that Biindigen Washk.

The neighbours, they act nice, and they say, "Oh, yes, yes, yes. You are sooooooo right. It will never happen again. You can trust us."

Then, whoops—it happens again. So those Nishnaabeg had those neighbours over for dinner, try and come up with some ground rules.

The neighbours, they act nice, and they say, "Oh, yes, yes, yes. You are sooooooo right. It will never happen again. You can trust us."

Then, whoops, it happens again. So the Nishnaabeg invite them over one more time for a serious discussion with no pie. Just tea this time.

This time those neighbours say, "Whoa, whoa. What you people getting all in a knot for? What you people doing being so uptight all the time? We are just living our lives. Doing our thing. We can't stop trampling all your medicines or our economy fall apart and we'll have no health care and we'll get sick. You don't want us to get sick, do you, Nishnaabeg?"

Nishnaabeg don't want anyone to get sick. Sick is no fun.

"Everything is going to be okay, Nishnaabeg," those neighbours say.

"We do better. See? Your plants, they're not so trampled. They're already coming back. You're making a big deal about nothing. We'll be more careful. It won't happen again."

Then, whoops, it happens again. And those neighbours go and plant a lawn and geraniums right on top of where Nishnaabe medicines are supposed to be.

Nishnaabeg start to get mad. They start to think that those neighbours are not honourable. Maybe those neighbours are doing a bit of lying. Maybe those neighbours are trying to pull the wool over those Nishnaabeg eyes.

So they have a big meeting, and they don't invite the neighbours this time. Nimkiig Binesiwag watches from above. Everybody has ideas about what to do. But which idea is going to work? That's always the problem.

Somebody says, "This idea going to work, this is the way to go, I'm sure of it."

Then a woman says, "What about this? You forgot about this. This is going to be a problem."

It goes around like that for a long time.

Every time they get close to deciding, a particular Niimkii Binesi, Echo-maker, flies over the meeting, booming and crashing, saying, "No, no, no. Don't decide when you're all mad. Don't decide too quick. Take your time on this one. Sleep on it. Go get massages first. Then decide. Everybody acts nice after massages. Clears the head and heart."

So those Nishnaabeg go and get massages. The real nice kind with dim lights and new-age music and flannel sheets.

In the meantime, though, those Nimkiig Binesiwag have their own meeting. They know that big pot of really-bad-medicine-soup is leaking and they know who they need to talk with. Except she is kinda snippy sometimes, that one. She does good work, but sometimes Nimkiig Binesiwag maybe get a little jealous or offended, or maybe that one that lives in the water maybe gets a little snippy and then next thing you know someone throws a rock or someone gets called a *monster* and then maybe a fight gets on.

So Nimkiig Binesiwag have to be careful. They have to go carefully down to that beach and give her name a call, all sweet like, "Mishibizhiw,"—or maybe her nickname, "Bizhiw." Maybe put out an offering. Maybe sing that song she likes, about the time First Striker didn't duck fast enough and lost a tail feather. Maybe she'll sing that one just to get her in a cushy mood.

But, while the Nimkiig Binesiwag are talking and deciding and taking their time, and, while Echo-maker is flying around trying to get those Nishnaabeg to their massages before they make a bad decision, Overseer goes down to the beach, puts an offering down, and sings that song. Overseer is an old and wise Nimkii Binesi, I'll tell you that. She's been around the block a few times and knows what she's doing.

Then she waits.

SHE WAITS AND WAITS.

SHE WAITS AND WAITS AND WAITS.

SHE WAITS SOME MORE.

Then she starts to get impatient. Like maybe Bizhiw is there and just not coming up so she can see her. Maybe she's even making her wait on purpose.

Overseer flies over the water to see what she can see. See if she can see any signs.

The water gets all choppy, and the wind gets all excited like maybe something is going to happen. Then, the sky gets all dark and grey-coloured.

"HOLA, what happened to my sunny day? NIMKIIG BINESI-WAG, gimme my sunny day back! I'm working on my tan because I have a hot date tonight. Got a new fancy party dress, going to that new place to eat, and I WANT MY SUNNY DAY BACK!" yells Bizhiw.

"Oh, why, Aaniin, Bizhiw, so nice to see you. I bet you gonna look some kinda fine in that new party dress. I'll give you your sunny day back, don't you worry. You'll get your sunny day back in time for your tan and your date. But first, I need you to do something for me."

Overseer gets out some candy and gives it to Bizhiw. Everybody wants to be a helper after candy.

Then Overseer butters Bizhiw up: "This job is really, really important. The survival of the lake depends upon it. The survival of the Nishnaabeg depends upon it. The survival of Bizhiwag and Binesiwag depend upon it. And you, Bizhiw, are the only one smart enough, fast enough, and with enough sucking power to do it."

Bizhiw eats up the candy. "Hey, Overseer, how about licorice next time. Red, not the black."

"Okay, Bizhiw, next time licorice."

Bizhiw thinks about Overseer's request. "I am really fast. And I am very smart, and nobody—I mean NOOOOOBODY—can suck like me. It's true."

"Yep, it is. Now pay attention. I need you to swim down the river. They just dredged it out, and there is lots of deep. Swim down that river until you get to the bridge. Then take a hard left."

"But there is no hard left."

"True, you are going to have to dig."

"Dig? I just got my nails done. I am not digging. Like the colour?"

"Oh, yes. The colour is perfect. Blueberry, na?"

"Ehn, it's blueberries all right."

"I'll fix your nails after the dig, okay? My auntie does nails; I'll get you a special deal. No problem. She does feet too. Okay?"

"Okay. So you take a hard left and dig horizontal, like, for maybe 500 metres. Then you going to be right at the big pot of really-bad-medicine-soup."

"Okay, then what?"

"Then you suck and suck and suck. Suck all that really bad medicine out of the big pot. Till it's gone."

"Okay."

"Okay."

"Overseer?"

"Yep?"

"Do I got time for a little fun on the way home after all that sucking?"

"Like what?"

"Maybe knock down that machine that makes all the birchbark?"

"I dunno. That's going to make the neighbours really mad."

"The neighbours are already really mad because that soup they were making is all gone."

"Okay. Maybe hit it by mistake with your tail on the way back out. Then call me; I'll set that appointment up with my auntie for your nails and feet. I'll get you a real bargain."

The next day, those Nishnaabeg are coming out of Echo-maker's Massage Therapy Clinic, when they see some kind of strange blue light off in the distance. It's at the base of the mountain, sort of imploding and maybe getting sucked into the ground, like a big vacuum just under the surface. Their eyes are a little blurry from all that dim light and that padded toilet seat you put your face in at the massage place. They think they not seeing right.

But when they get home, the neighbours all gone. No house, no lawn, no geraniums, no fence even. Like they were never there. Like they are under a large invisibility cloak or something. Erased. Gone. Kaput. Maybe it was all just a bad dream. The Nishnaabeg sit down in their house all relaxed, have some tea, maybe a snack. Try to remember what they were doing before those neighbours showed up.

Nishnaabemowin: Nimkiig Binesiwag are thunderbirds, in some areas people just say "Binesiwag," in others they just say "Nimkiig," and sometimes it is a combination of the two; nahow means okay; semaa (asemaa) is tobacco; biindigen washk is rhubarb; Bizhiw is lynx and is a reference to Mishibizhiw, the underwater lynx; bizhiwag are lynxes.

10

WANT

Sometimes our Elders and storytellers talk about Wiindigoog. Wiindigoo is a kind of monster who is always hungry, and, no matter what Wiindigoo eats, she never feels full. No matter how many toys Wiindigoo has, he always wants more. No matter how many trees Wiindigoo cuts down to make into paper, Wiindigoo always wants to cut down more. No matter how many lego sets Wiindigoo has, he always needs one more. Wiindigoo always wants more.

This can be kind of a problem for Wiindigoog; Wiindigoog are so hungry that they are always trying to snack on things that would rather not be snacked on. Some people say that the problem is that they have a lot of want inside them, and their want is always growing bigger and bigger.

One day, along time ago, in dagwaagin, the Wiindigoog were planning on making a snack out of Nanabush and Nokomis. Zhagashkaandawe, the flying squirrel, overheard the Wiindigoog plans, and she went directly to Nanabush to warn her.

But Nanabush was sleeping.

"Wake up, Nanabush! Wake up!" shouted Zhagashkaandawe.

Nanabush kept on snoring.

Zhagashkaandawe tried again in her loudest, most yelly, outside voice.

"WAKE UP NANABUSH!"

But Nanabush just kept on snoring.

Zhagashkaandawe was getting worried, so she got tricky. She went outside and collected some pine cones. Then she crawled to the top of the lodge and dropped them on old Nanabush's face.

"Yeeeoowwww!" screamed Nanabush. "What is going on here?"

Zhagashkaandawe spoke quickly and clearly and told Nanabush of the Wiindigoog plan.

Nanabush was immediately concerned because she knew Nokomis was getting old, and quick travel was hard for her. But Zhagashkaandawe had an idea. "I know a place where Nokomis can hide. On the other side of the big waterfall is a beautiful maple forest. It can only be reached by crossing over the river on a log. The Ninaatigoog will take care of Nokomis."

"Miigwech, Zhagashkaandawe! That is a good idea," Nanabush said, leaving a pile of hazelnuts for that squirrel. She set off for Nokomis's camp to tell her about the Wiindigoog snack plan.

When Nokomis heard the news, she immediately began to roll the birchbark up to her lodge. She packed up her things, put her pack on, and they set off towards the waterfall. When they got to the Ninaatigoog, Nanabush built a new lodge, and Nokomis put her sheets of birchbark around it.

The Wiindigoog were not too far behind Nanabush and Nokomis, but, when they got to the waterfall, they stopped dead in their tracks. The Ninaatigoog appeared to be engulfed in a raging fire. The Wiindigoog talked amongst themselves. They decided on something different for their snack, leaving Nanabush and Nokomis alone.

You see, the Ninaatigoog were in their fall colours, so, when the Wiindigoog looked across the river, what they thought was fire was really the crimson-red colour of the trees. What they thought was smoke was really mist from the waterfall. They had been fooled by the maple trees. The Ninaatigoog had been a nest of safety for Nanabush and Nokomis.

Nanabush was very thankful to the Ninaatigoog, so she made their sap very sweet. Even today, the Nishnaabeg feel very safe and happy when we are in the sugar bush, just like Nokomis and Nanabush so long ago felt. Even today—no, *especially* today—the

Nishnaabeg think about how unbalanced things can get when the want inside us gets out of control.

Nishnaabemowin: Wiindigoog is the plural of Wiinidigo and refers to a kind of monster; dawaagin is the fall; zhagashkaandawe is a flying squirrel; and ninaatigoog (ininatigoog) are maple trees.

11

ZHIGAAG'S POWERFUL MEDICINE

"Nbakade! Nbakade! Nbakade!" Nanabush yelled. "I'm hungry!"

Hunting seemed like too much work. Fishing seemed like too much work. Snaring rabbits seemed like too much work. Ricing had seemed like too much work last fall, so Nanabush didn't put any in his cache. The maple sugar from last spring was too good to save; Nanabush had already gobbled his up. There were no berries or roots or plants to be seen.

"Nbakade!"

"That Zhigaag never seems to do much work," thought Nanabush. "I never see her working too hard, but she always has food to eat. Hmmmmm."

"Zhigaag! Zhigaag!" Nanabush hollered as he went off to find Skunk.

Finding her sleeping in her den, Nanabush called, "Zhigaag, I need some of your skunk medicine. I'm hungry and lazy, and I think you have all this skunk medicine, and you should share."

"Hmmm," thought Zhigaag. "It is a very good thing to share, and I can see that you are very hungry. But my skunk medicine is powerful, and it takes a long time to learn how to use it. You have to be careful."

"I am very, very good at being careful," replied Nanabush. "Exceptionally good, really."

"Nahow. I'll share, but you have to agree to follow my instructions. No tricks," said Zhigaag.

Nanabush passed Zhigaag his semaa. "Yes, yes, yes," he said. "I am also very good at following instructions. I follow them right down to the letter. I never make mistakes. You can count on me."

Zhigaag wasn't so sure. "Are you sure, Nanabush? Are you sure you can follow my instructions?"

"Ehn! Ehn! Ehn! No worries, Zhigaag."

So Zhigaag lifted her tail and transferred the skunk medicine into Nanabush's butt. Oh, that Nanabush thought he was something now, with all that skunk power. Zhigaag told him to go to his lodge and play his drum until Mooz showed up. She said that he could use his new skunk medicine on the Mooz and have a big feast. Nanabush thanked Zhigaag and started to walk to his lodge, all proud with his new skunk power.

Pretty soon, he thought he should at least test it out and see if it was working. He decided to boogidi some skunk medicine out at a tree, just as a test, and CABOOM! The tree exploded.

"SHTAA SHTAA TAA HAA!" shouted Nanabush. "This is AWESOME!"

Pretty soon, he thought that the last test might have been a fluke, at least scientifically. So, he did another boogidi, and skunk medicine flew out at a lake, and CABOOM! A beautiful fountain of water appeared.

"SHTAA SHTAA TAA HAA!" shouted Nanabush. "This is AMAZING!"

Pretty soon, he thought, "Let's try best two out of three." CABOOM! A rock exploded into dust.

"SHTAA TAA HAA!" shouted Nanabush. "This is WICKED!"

Pretty soon, he thought, "Really, it is four that is the sacred number. I can't really just stop at three because that would be so unbalanced. Things come in fours for the Nishnaabeg."

So, he did a boogidi, and skunk medicine flew out at Beaver's lodge, and CABOOM! The logs were up in the air, scattered everywhere. They even fell to the ground in a perfectly stacked woodpile.

"SHTAA SHTAA TAA HAA!" shouted Nanabush. "This is SO ROCK AND ROLL!"

Then Nanabush continued on to his lodge. He sat and played his drum, just as Zhigaag had instructed, and pretty soon Mooz showed up, just as Zhigaag had said he would.

Nanabush turned around and farted out his skunk medicine, but nothing happened. He tried again and again and again. They were just regular old farts, no Zhigaag.

Mooz waited around to see if Nanabush could get his act together, but after a while Mooz got bored and left, and Nanabush had to go back to hunting the hard way. But he remembered this event for a long, long time. He carried it in his bones, and the next time someone gave him instructions, he tried his very best to be responsible.

Nishnaabemowin: Zhigaag is skunk; nahow is okay; semaa (asemaa) is tobacco; ehn means yes; boogijizh is to fart, literally spray, or do as the skunk does; boogidi is a fart; shtaa taa haa! means awesome; mooz is moose.

12

THE PLACE OF MUDDY WATER

In the fall, dagwaagin, the Nishnaabeg, are busy getting ready for bboon. They are out on the lake ricing, smoking fish, drying berries, harvesting their vegetables and medicines—getting all the food they will need for the winter cached.

This dagwaagin, however, Nanabush is gitimi, he is feeling kind of lazy.

"Oh, the winter is so hard," he complained. "It is so hard to hunt. Ice fishing is so boring. The wind is so cold. The nights are so long. Winter is so much work."

Just then, a flock of Nikag flew overhead in a V, heading to Zhaawanong for the winter.

"Hmmmmm," thought Nanabush. "It would be kind of nice to spend the winter in Zhaawanong. Fishing would be easy with the ocean right there. I could spend most of my time just lying on the beach!"

So Nanabush headed down to the minomiin beds to wait for the Nikag to land.

"Aaniin, Gimaa Nika," Nanabush said to the leader of the geese.

"Aaniin, Nanabush," she said back.

"I see you are flying to Zhaawanong. Oh, yes, very good for you. I'm sure it will be very warm and sunny in Florida. I'm sure you'll have a great time on the beach with all the sun and the sand and the sea. You see, I was wondering if I might come along with you this year. I am old and tired, and I can't possibly go through another winter here."

Gimaa Nika felt suspicious. She remembered what happened to the Zhiishiibag when Nanabush tricked them into being dinner with a blindfold and a dance.

"Ehn, Zhaawanong is beautiful. But, Nanabush, you can't even fly," replied Gimaa Nika.

Nanabush needed to butter Nikag up a little bit. "But, Gimaa, your nation is so strong and powerful. Your wings and navigation are top-notch. I am sure all together you could fly me to Zhawnong."

"I'll speak to my people," said Gimaa, wondering what Nanabush had planned.

The Nikag had a big meeting. Everyone showed up—moms, dads, children, aunties, uncles, grandparents, brothers, sisters, sons, and daughters. They all spoke what was in their hearts and minds. Then they sent Gimaa Nika back to tell Nanabush their decision.

"Nanabush, my people have decided that you may come with us to Zhaawanong, as long as you follow our three rules."

"That's perfect!" shouted Nanabush. "I LOVE rules, and I am very, very good at following them right down to the letter! I've recently learned from Zhigaag what can happen if you stretch the rules a bit, so I'm all back to following them. I've turned over a new leaf, really."

"Okay. Rule number one is NO TALKING. Rule number two is NO TRICKS. Rule number three is NO LOOKING DOWN."

"Ehn! Ehn! Ehn!" responded Nanabush. "Those rules are super easy. This is going to be fantastic. When do we leave?"

"If you break the rules, Nanabush, we are going to drop you. If there are tricks in Zhaawanong, Nanabush, we are going to leave you there, and you'll have to walk home. Meet us here tomorrow at dawn."

"This is no problem at all. I've got to go home and pack and make some snacks for the road trip! Baamaa aapii!"

The next morning they left, and even though Nanabush had over-packed, the flight to Zhaawanong was pretty good.

Nanabush followed all of the in-flight rules. All winter long they all had a wonderful time in the south visiting with those southern relations, learning about their lands and nations.

Soon it was time to return to Giiwedinong. The Nikag came to where Nanabush was staying and picked him up for his flight home.

Nanabush was pretty excited about going home. Spring was his favourite time. He knew the Nishnaabeg would be busy in the sugar bush, hunting muskrat, and spear fishing, and he could not wait to see all of his friends and relations. The closer he got, the more excited he felt. He was so excited, his body was shaking. Still, the Nikag held on tight to him as they flew north.

When he reached the land of the Nishnaabeg, he was so excited he could barely stay still. Then he heard the Nishnaabeg say, "Look up in the sky, it's Nanabush flying with the geese!"

Looking down, he waved at his friends and relatives proudly. And the geese let go of him.

Nanabush fell to the earth and landed with a thud. Reaching around for the hard ground, he instead felt soft fur. Reaching around for the cold rocks, he instead felt warmth. Listening for the quiet of the spring morning, he instead heard loud snoring.

"Who is interrupting my nap? Who is lying on top of me? What is that weird smell?" exclaimed a sleepy Makwa.

Quickly Nanabush scrambled to his feet and out of the Makweesh, and he ran as fast as he could towards the Nishnaabeg. He couldn't wait to tell them all about his fantastic adventures.

The next dagwaagin, Nanabush was feeling kind of lazy and not paying attention to things. He had forgotten all about what happened last winter.

"Oh, the winter is so hard. It is so hard to hunt. Ice fishing is so boring. The wind is so cold. The nights are so long. Winter is so much work."

Just then, a flock of Nikag flew overhead in a V, heading to Zhaawanong for the winter.

"Hmmmmm," thought Nanabush. "It would be kind of nice to spend the winter in Zhaawanong. Fishing would be easy with the ocean right there. I could spend most of my time just lying on the beach!"

So Nanabush headed down to the minomiin beds to wait for the Nikag to land.

"Aaniin, Gimaa Nika," Nanabush said to the leader of the geese.

"Aaniin, Nanabush," she said back.

"I see you are flying to Zhaawanong. Oh, yes, very good for you. I'm sure it will be very warm and sunny in Florida. I'm sure you'll have a great time on the beach with all the sun and the sand and the sea. You see, I was wondering if I might come along with you this year. I am old and tired, and I can't possibly go through another winter here."

Gimaa Nika felt suspicious. She remembered what happened last spring.

"Ehn, Zhaawanong is beautiful. But, Nanabush, last spring, you didn't follow the rules," replied Gimaa Nika.

Nanabush realized he needed to butter Nikag Gimaa up a little bit.

"But, Gimaa, your nation is so strong and powerful. Your wings and navigation are high-end. I am sure together you could fly me to Zhaawanong. I am sure this time I can follow your rules!"

"I'll speak to my people," said Gimaa.

The Nikag had a big meeting. Everyone showed up—moms, dads, children, aunties, uncles, grandparents, brothers, sisters, sons, and daughters. They all spoke what was in their hearts and minds. Then they sent Gimaa Nika back to tell Nanabush their decision.

"Nanabush, my people have reluctantly decided that you may come with us to Zhaawanong. But you MUST follow the three rules. We are going to give you one more chance."

LEANNE SIMPSON

"That's perfect!" shouted Nanabush, "I LOVE rules and I am very, very good at following them right down to the letter!"

"Okay. Let's go over this one more time. Rule number one is NO TALKING. Rule number two is NO TRICKS. Rule number three is NO LOOKING DOWN."

"Ehn! Ehn! Ehn!" responded Nanabush. "Those rules are super easy. This is going to be fantastic. When do we leave?"

"If you break the rules, Nanabush, we are going to drop you. If there are tricks in Zhaawanong, Nanabush, we are going to leave you there and you'll have to walk home. Meet us here tomorrow at dawn."

"This is no problem at all. I've got to go home and pack and make some snacks for the road trip! Baamaa aapii!"

The next morning they left, and even though Nanabush had over-packed, the flight to Zhaawanong was pretty good. Nanabush followed all of the in-flight rules. All winter long they all had a wonderful time in the south visiting with those southern relations, learning about their lands and nations.

Soon it was time to return to Giiwedinong, and the Nikag came to where Nanabush was staying and picked him up for his flight home.

Nanabush was pretty excited about going home. Spring was his favourite time. He knew the Nishnaabeg would be busy in the sugar bush, hunting muskrat and spear fishing, and he could not wait to see all of his friends and relations. The closer he got, the more excited he felt. He was so excited, his body was shaking. He needed to take a little peek just to see how much longer the trip was going to take. Just a little peek.

Boom! Nanabush fell to the ground.

Instead of hitting the ground hard, though, Nanabush fell into a muddy marsh. The landing was pretty good, considering, but he was then covered from head to toe with thick mud. He had to get himself fixed up before the Nishnaabeg saw him!

Nanabush ran to the nearest lake. The water was freezing because the ice was barely off, but he jumped in anyway and kicked and splashed around until he was shiny.

Nanabush got dressed and looked at the lake. It was muddy. It was very muddy. It was so muddy that Nanabush thought it would never be clear again.

"I'm going to name this lake Wiin nibii aang," said Nanabush, "the place of muddy water."

And people today call that place Lake Winnipeg.

Nishnaabemowin: Dagwaagin is the fall; bboon is winter; gitimi means s/he is lazy; zhaawanong is the south; aaniin means hello in Mississauga Nishnaabemowin; minomiin (manomiin in other parts of the territory) is wild rice; nika is a goose; nikag is geese; Gimaa (Ogimaa) is Chief or leader; zhiishiibag is ducks; ehn is yes; baamaa aapii is see you later; makweesh is bear den.

It's a Very Good Thing to Be Yourself

There are a lot of good stories and good songs about old Baapaase, Woodpecker.

There is the one about Baapaase always telling everyone else's stories before anyone else could tell them. In that one, Nanabush gives Baapaase a very loud knocking sound so that everyone will know when Baapaase is coming.

There is the one about Baapaase helping Nanabush and Nanabush giving her a beautiful red crest as a thank you.

There is the one about Baapaase helping Nokomis teach everyone about sharing. Owah! That's a good one too.

But this one, this one is more about Nanabush than Baapaase. One day, a long time ago, Nanabush was in the forest, and, of course, he was feeling hungry.

"Nbakade! Nbakade! Nbakade!" he yelled and then listened.

Knock. Knock. Knock. Knock.Knock. Knock. Knock.Knock. Knock. Knock.

All day long, knocking!

Then Nanabush watched. She saw Baapaase flying from tree to tree, knocking on each tree with her beak and then eating. The very loudest tree in the woods was even named after Baapaase, Baapaagamag, the White Ash.

Nanabush watched some more.

"That looks pretty easy. Pretty easy," thought Nanabush.

She got to work right away. She carved a beak out of cedar. She made straps out of leather and then attached her Baapaase face to her Nanabush face and climbed up a tree.

When she was near the top, she tipped his head back and then smashed it into the trunk as hard as she could.

"OUCH! AHHHHHHHHHHHHH!" she screamed. "OOOOOOOOOOWWWWWWWWWEEEEEEEE!"

Nanabush fell to the ground with a thud and screamed, "AHHHHHHHHHHHH!"

Nokomis came to see what all the commotion was about.

"Nanabush, are you all right? What were you doing? Why are you on the ground? Why is your face all bloody and your nose blown up like a red balloon?"

"Oh, Nokomis," Nanabush snivelled. "I thought Baapaase had it so easy gathering food as easy as pie, so I made a face just like hers and I tried it and this is what happened."

"My Nanabush," Nokomis said, giving Nanabush a big, warm Nokomis hug. "It didn't work because you are not a Baapaase. You are a Nanabush, and a Nanabush is a very good thing to be. There is no one else in the world like you."

Then she took her Nanabush home and cleaned up her face and gave her some nice warm soup, because a Nokomis is also a very nice thing to be.

Nishnaabemowin: Baapaase is a woodpecker; Nbakade means I'm hungry; Baapaagamag, the White Ash.

14

Honouring Ojiig
in the Night Sky

One day Ojiig was out hunting with his Daanis.

Ojiigag are great hunters, but life was very difficult at this time because it was always bboon. Always. No spring. No summer. No fall. Only bboon.

One day, Daanis and Ojiig are out hunting and hunting and hunting, and finally Daanis, even though she is very tough, has had enough.

"Ojiig, I am freezing," she says. "I can't stop shivering. I don't think I can go on."

"Oh, my Daanis," Ojiigag says, looking ahead and into the snow. "I can see things are so very difficult for you, but we must keep going and find some food for our family."

"Nahow, Ojiig. But isn't there anything you can do to bring some warmth to our land?"

Well, this happened to be a very good question. It had been bboon for so long, though, that no one else had even thought to ask if warmth was possible!

Ojiig thought for a minute, then interrupted the silence. "Let's get everyone together and see if anyone can remember a time when the land was warm."

That is exactly what they did. All the animals came. The old ones brought their pipes. The young ones helped to smudge. Everyone thought and listened and tried to remember. After a long time, and together, they decided that the warmth must be in the Sky World.

Ojiig, Nigig, Bizhiw, and Gwiingwa'aage volunteered to go on the journey to the Sky World. After prayers and ceremony, they left, heading for the epingishimog. They travelled across the deep snow of the forest and the prairies until they came to the tallest mountain. Then, they climbed up that mountain to get as close as possible to Giizhik.

Nigig jumped first, but he jumped with such force that he busted right through the sky. He hit the ground hard, sliding all the way down the mountain.

Bizhiw tried next, but when he jumped he knocked his head so hard on Giizhik that he lost consciousness.

"Gwiingwa'aage!" exclaimed Ojiig. "You are the strongest among us. You are our last hope!"

Gwiingwa'aage did little pogo-stick bounces towards Giizhik again and again and again, until she cracked open a tiny hole. The three relatives jumped through the small hole together. Gwiingwa'aage jumped through the hole in the Giizhik, with Ojiig close behind.

The Sky World was beautiful. It was warm and lush where trees, medicines, and flowers grew. Gwiingwa'aage and Ojiig worked together to make the hole bigger so the warmth of the Sky World would flow down to their mother.

After they worked for a long time, the snow started to melt, the waters started to flow, and the world began to wake up. Gwiingwa'aage and Ojiig continued to make the hole bigger and bigger.

Finally, a little Sky-Kwezens asked them to stop. "Excuse me, you are making a big hole in my world. Why? I'd like you to stop because my world is losing a lot of heat and light, please and thank you very much."

Gwiingwa'aage was so startled, she fell all the way back to earth. Ojiig and Sky-Kwezens decided that, if they made the hole the right size, both worlds could share the heat and light at the same time. Ojiig chewed at the hole to make it just the right size.

But some of the Sky people weren't as kind as Sky-Kwezens. These beings started to chase Ojiig with their arrows. One struck her and made her fall backwards to the earth.

Gzhwe Manidoo watched all of this. Honouring her for her work, the Creator picked up Ojiig and placed her in the stars for trying to help everyone on earth. So, while a lot of people look up in the sky and see the Big Dipper, the Nishnaabeg look up and see Ojiig, the great hunter. Every winter Ojiig is struck by the arrow and falls over on her back, but during the summer she rolls onto her feet to bring warmth back to her people.

And one more thing: Gwiingwa'aage has a really special name. Gwiingwa means a shooting star, and 'aage means emerging from. A long, long time ago, four crazy stars were racing towards the earth. Things got a little out of hand, and one of the stars crashed into the earth, making a big crater. Eventually, that crater filled up with water. After even more time, vegetation started to grow around it. After even more time still, the trees grew, and it eventually looked like any other lake. One day, out of that new pristine lake, a creature crawled out of the water, and that's the one we call Gwiingwa'aage, Wolverine—the one that emerged from a shooting star.

Nishnaabemowin: Ojiig is a fisher; daanis means daughter; bizhiw is a lynx; nigig is an otter; bboon is winter; nahow means okay; eping-ishimog means west; gizhiik is sky; kwezens (ikwezens) is a girl; and gwiingwa'aage is a wolverine, the one that emerged from a shooting star; Gzhwe Manidoo is the Creator, the one who loves us unconditionally.

15

GWIIWZENS MAKES A LOVELY DISCOVERY

Gwiiwzens is out walking in the bush one day
It is Ziigwan
the lake is opening up
the goon is finally melting
he's feeling that first warmth of spring on his cheeks. "Nigitchi
nendam," he is thinking, "I'm happy."

Then that Gwiiwzens, who is out walking
collecting firewood for his Doodoom
decides to sit under Ninaatigoog
maybe just stretch out
maybe just have a little rest
maybe gather firewood a little later.
"Oowah, Ngitchi nendam nongom,"
"I'm feeling happy today," says that Gwiiwzens.

And, while that Gwiiwzens
is lying down, and looking up
he sees San'goo up in the tree
"Bozhoo, San'goo! I hope you had a good winter.
I hope you had enough food cached."
But San'goo doesn't look down because she's already busy.
She's not collecting nuts.
Gawiin.
She's not building her nest

Gawiin, not yet.
She's not looking after any young.
Gawiin, too early.
She's just nibbling on the bark, and then doing some sucking.

    Nibble, nibble suck.
    Nibble, nibble suck.
    Nibble, nibble, suck.
    Nibble, nibble, suck.

Gwiiwzens is feeling a little curious.
So he does it too, on one of the low branches.

    Nibble, nibble suck.
    Nibble, nibble suck.
    Nibble, nibble, suck.
    Nibble, nibble, suck.

Mmmmmmmmmmmmmm.
This stuff tastes good.
It's real, sweet water.
Mmmmmmmmmmmmm.

Then Gwiiwzens gets thinking
and he makes a hole in that tree
and he makes a little slide for
that sweet water to run down
he makes a quick little container
out of birchbark, and
he collects that sweet water
and he takes that sweet water home
to show his mama.

That doodoom is excited, and she has three hundred questions:

"Ah, Gwiiwzens, what is this?"
"Where did you find it?"
"Which tree?"

"Who taught you how to make it?"
"Did you put semaa?"
"Did you say miigwech?"
"How fast is it dripping?"
"Does it happen all day?"
"Does it happen all night?"
"Where's the firewood?"

Gwiiwzens tells his doodoom the story.
She believes every word
because he is her Gwiiwzens
and they love each other very much.
"Let's cook the meat in it tonight,
it will be lovely sweet."
"Nahow."
"Nahow."

So they cooked that meat in that sweet water
it was lovely sweet
it was extra lovely sweet
it was even sweeter than just that sweet water.

The next day, Gwiiwzens takes his mama
to that tree, and his mama brings Nokomis
and Nokomis brings all the aunties, and
there is a very big crowd of Nishnaabekwewag
and there is a very big lot of pressure
Gwiiwzens tells about San'goo.
Gwiiwzens does the nibble-nibble-suck part.

At first there are technical difficulties
and none of it works.
But Mama rubs Gwiiwzen's back
she tells Gwiiwzens that she believes him anyway
they talk about lots of variables, like heat and temperature
and time
then Giizis comes out and warms everything up
and soon it's drip

     drip
        drip
           drip

those aunties go crazy
Saasaakwe!
dancing around
hugging a bit too tight
high kicking
and high fiving
until they take it back home
boil it up
boil it down
into sweet, sweet sugar.

Ever since, every Ziigwan
those Nishnaabekwewag
collect that sweet water
and boil it up
and boil it down
into that sweet, sweet sugar
all thanks to Gwiiwzens and his lovely discovery

    and to San'goo and her precious teaching
      and to Ninaatigoog and their boundless sharing.

Nishnaabemowin: Gwiiwzens (gwiiwizens) means a boy; ziigwan is the early part of spring when the snow is melting, the ice is breaking up, and the sap is flowing; nigitchi nendam means I am happy; doodoom is one of our very old names for mama; "doodoo" means breast milk; ninaatigoog are maple trees; san'goo is a black squirrel; bozhoo is hello; gawiin is no; semaa (asemaa) is tobacco; miigwech is thank you; nahow is okay; saasaakwe is a yell of approval; Nishnaabekwewag is women; and giizis is sun.

16

THE STAR PEOPLE
ARE ALWAYS WATCHING

A long, long time ago, Gwiiwzens was looking up at the sky at night and he noticed a new anang. It was very bright, and, as soon as he saw it, he ran and told his grandparents. His grandparents gathered all the Elders together, and they all agreed: there was a new anang in the sky. No one had ever seen it before.

Everyone had a lot of questions. What should we do? Is it a sign? Is it a message? Why is the new anang here? What has this anang come to tell us?

After a long discussion, the Elders decided to ask Migizi to fly as high as she could, and when she is as high as she could possibly go, Migizi would ask that anang why she was here.

Migizi prepared for her big flight. She ate lots and lots of gigoonhag. She slept. She got her nest in order, and then she left, flying higher and higher than she ever had. She stopped and rested on the tallest mountain in the land. Then she flew higher.

When she couldn't fly any more, she called out, "Shki Anang, why are you here? What do you want?"

Shki Anang answered, "I have been watching the Nishnaabeg for many moons now. They are so happy. They are so gentle with their children. They have great respect for their Elders. I love how they all work together and take care of each other. I want to come and live with them."

"Miigwech," said Migizi. "I will take your request back to my people."

When Migizi returned to Gchi Nishnaabeg-ogaming, he told the people what Shki Anang had said. Everyone listened very carefully. After Migizi was done relaying the message from Shki Anang, the people went back to their families to discuss what she had said.

Soon, they all agreed that it would be a good idea for Shki Anang to come and live amongst them. They thought maybe the mountain would be a good place for her to live.

Migizi told Shki Anang the good news, and she came down out of the sky to make her home on the mountain. She could sure see what the Nishnaabeg were doing, up so high on that mountain, but she longed to hear their voices. She still felt lonely for them. Shki Anang asked the people if she could move to the bush.

The Nishnaabeg went back to their families to discuss this new idea, and pretty soon everyone agreed. Shki Anang moved to the bush.

At first the bush was great. Shki Anang could certainly hear the Nishnaabeg, but, once the leaves came out on the trees, she couldn't see them. She went back to the Sky World to think about this problem. How was she ever going to be able to be with her beloved people? The Sky People listened to her problem and talked again until Dibik Giizis came up with the perfect idea.

Shki Anang descended back to the land of the Nishnaabeg, this time landing gracefully on the water. She spread her arms and legs out so she floated, and she became the most beautiful water lily.

After that, the Nishnaabeg gave her a new name: Nibiish Waawaasgone, Water Flower. Nibiish Waawaasgone reminds the Nishnaabeg of the beautiful Sky World and her people, and she reminds us to always live in a careful, gentle, and loving way. In her thankfulness, Nibiish Waawaasgone often gives her roots so that powerful medicines can be made.

Nishnaabemowin: Nibiish Waawaaskgone is a water lily; gwiiwzens (gwiiwizens) means a boy; anang is a star; migizi is a bald eagle; gigoonh is fish; gigoonhag is more than one fish; shki-anang means the new star; miigwech means thank you; Gchi Nishnaabeg-ogaming means "the place where we live and work together" according to Elder Doug Williams from Curve Lake First Nation, and dibik giizis is the moon.

17

ZHIISHIIB MAKES EVERYBODY LUNCH

One time a long, long, long time ago
there was this old Nokomis
and she was camped by the side of a lake
not too far from here.
In dagwaagin.

Everyone was busy getting ready for bboon.
Fishing.
Hunting.
Moving camps.

Won't be long now.

One day, that old Nokomis was looking after her grandkids.
And it was warm and sunny
so she decided to paddle them to a beach for the last swim of
the year.
She packed their suits
and their towels
and their sand toys
and the sunscreen
and the sun hats
and the bug spray
and the stuffies and the special blankets
and the coats in case it was cold on the paddle home

and the life jackets and paddles
and that orange bucket with the whistle in it so the boat cops
don't give her no trouble
and the extra clothes for when kwezens falls in.

And then she packed up those kids, and they were off.

Oh, those kids were happy!
Splashing and swimming
in that dagwaagin sun.

"Oh, I've remembered everything," thought that Nokomis.
"I'm a multi-tasker. No one is more organized than me."
"I'm Nishnaaabe Martha Stewart."

And then that little kwezens said, "Kokum, nbakade!"
And Nokomis remembers she forgot to pack that blue cooler
full of lunch.

Nbakade! Nbakade!

Nokomis told those kids to calm down. Calm down.
You won't die because lunch is late.
And she went to sit on a rock.

Pretty soon, she saw Zhiishiib.

And that Zhiishiib had a kettle on the fire.

And in that akik on the shkode were some grains.

And so that Nokomis went over to Zhiishiib and offered some semaa.
And that Zhiishiib showed Nokomis how to knock the minomiin
and parch the minomiin
and dance the minomiin
and eat the minomiin.

And so Nokomis and her grandkids ate big bowls of manoomiin for lunch.

And that Nokomis went back to her camp, and she showed all the Nishnaabekwewag what she had learned.

And so, every year, those Nishnaabekwewag go out onto the lake just like Zhiishiib, and they knock that rice into their jiimaanan.

But they're very careful, because that minomiin is very sensitive. They make sure most of it goes back into the water so the ducks and the geese and the Nishnaabekwewag will have enough for next year. And then they share their minomiin, so that everyone can taste the lake all through the bboon.

And then they share that manoomiin, so that everyone can taste the lake all through bboon, right until it's time for Nishnaabekwewag to go and see ninaatagoog.

Nishnaabemowin: Minomiin-Giizis means wild rice moon and is in August or September, depending upon which part of our territory you are in; Dagwaagin means fall; bboon is the winter; Kwezens (ikwezens) is a girl; n'bakade means I'm hungry; zhiishiib means duck; Kookum is another name for Grandmother; akik is pail; shkode is fire; semaa (asemaa) is tobacco; jiimaanan are canoes; minomiin (manomiin in other parts of the territory) is wild rice; Nishnaabekwewag is Ojibwe women; and ninaatigoog means maple trees.

18

MAKWA, THE GREAT FASTER

Makwa, the great faster, the great dreamer, is usually asleep in bboon. Usually. Because Makwa, the great visionary, the potent medicine teacher, spends a great deal of time with the Spirits in the dream world, and that's why those bears are such powerful healers. Usually.

But, this one time, a very, very long time ago, he woke up in February, Makwa Giizis. Now, usually, when Makwa wakes up in Makwa Giizis, it is just to turn around in the den, just to get a bit more comfortable. Usually. But not this time. This time, he crawled out of his makweesh, and began sleepily wandering around the forest.

"Gi nibaa na? Are you sleeping?" asked Bizhiw.

"Gaawiin!" answered Makwa.

"Gi nibaa na? Are you sleeping?" asked Wabooz.

"Gaawiin!" answered Makwa.

"Gi nibaa na? Are you sleeping?" asked Wabzheshi.

"Gaawiin!" answered Makwa.

"Gi nibaa na? Are you sleeping?" asked Wagosh.

"Gaawiin!" answered Makwa.

Just then, though, Makwa noticed the big gigoonh that Wagosh was pulling.

"Wagosh, where did you get that lovely, big juicy fish?" he asked.

Wagosh explained how the Nishnaabeg had a hole in the ice out on the lake. He explained how to take a stick and push it through that ice on the surface to open up the hole. He explained how he turned around and used his tail as a fishing pole. Before long, the gigoonh chomped down on Wagosh's tail, and, when gigoonh did, Wagosh flicked his tail out of the hole and onto the lake, and, taa daa! she had caught the fish.

Makwa was impressed, and a tiny bit jealous. So Makwa decided to head down to the lake and catch his own gigoonh.

"Miigwech, Wagosh! Gaawaabmin miinawaa!" Makwa called, as he headed out onto the lake.

Makwa headed out onto the ice. It was the beginning of Makwa-Giizis, so the ice was very thick and very safe. He found the hole just like Wagosh had said, put his long, long tail in the hole, and he waited.

He waited

and waited

and waited

and waited, for what seemed like 358 years.

"Gsinaa!" said Makwa.

The water in the hole started to freeze. Makwa waited some more. No gigoonh.

Finally, Makwa gave up. He was very cold, very tired, and his tail was very frozen into the ice-fishing hole. He tried to get up but was stuck.

Makwa was getting frustrated and angry. He let out a big Makwa growl, and then he pushed up off the ice with all his strength. In the process, his tail broke right off, and his beautiful long tail became a beautiful short tail, just like the one he has today.

And so a pretty grumpy Makwa, with a pretty short, and sore, tail, lumbered off home to his den, because if there is one thing that bears do not do, it is ice fishing. Makwa, the great faster, the great dreamer, sleeps right through ice-fishing season.

Nishnaabemowin: Makwa is bear; bboon is winter; makweesh is bear den; Gi nibaa na? means are you sleeping?; bizhiw is lynx; gawiin means no; wabooz is rabbit; wabzheshi is martin; gigoonh is fish; miigwech means thank you; gwaabmin miinawaa means see you again; makwa-giizis is February; gisinaa—it is cold.

19

SHE HAD A BEAUTIFUL, SPECKLED DESIGN

A long, long time ago, some Michi Saagiig Anishinaabeg were living on an island in Lake Ontario for the Niibin. They were fishing and collecting medicines. They spent time berry picking and swimming. They visited each other and conducted their summer ceremonies.

In the middle of this island was a beautiful, clear, deep lake. It was the most beautiful colour of blue, and it was always sparkling, even on cloudy days. The lake was full of trout, but the Nishnaabeg knew this lake was special, so they never ate the fish from the lake in the middle of the island. They only ate the fish from the big lake, Chi'Nibiish.

Sometimes, the Nishnaabeg needed to paddle to the mainland to visit their relatives or to get a different kind of food. One day, the families decided to go to the mainland, and everyone was excited to go, except for Kwezens. She wanted to stay. Kwezens was an artist. She loved to bead beautiful patterns onto makizinan and paint beautiful designs onto her clothes. She loved to sew new clothes for her family. So her family took this into consideration. They thought that maybe she'd like the time to dream some new designs or finish some of the projects she'd been working on.

After a long discussion, the family agreed that Kwezens was old enough to stay by herself. Before they left, Kokum gently reminded Kwezens not to eat the fish from the lake in the middle of the island. Kwezens smiled and told Kokum she wouldn't forget. So the people loaded their jimaanan and set off for the mainland.

Kwezens felt free. She had the entire day to herself. Would she swim? Would she lie on the beach? Would she fish? Would she sew?

Kwezens also felt curious, very curious. So curious that she couldn't follow Kokum's reminder. So she went to the lake with her spear, and she caught one of the lake trout. She cleaned it and roasted it on the fire, and then she ate it.

When her family returned, they looked everywhere for Kwezens. They found her spear and her beading tools, but they couldn't find her.

After it was clear that Kwezens was gone, Kokum went to the lake in the middle of the island. She put some semaa into the water. She prayed and sang for Kwezens. She put a little bit of food into the lake, and soon a little trout appeared. But this trout wasn't like the others. She wasn't plain. She had a beautiful speckled design all over her body. Beautiful red dots surrounded by yellow haloes, just like the clothes Kwezens has been wearing. Before long, the lake was full of beautiful speckled trout with red dots and yellow haloes, and before long, the beautiful speckled trout found other lakes to live in too, and they were always happy to feed the Nishnaabeg.

Nishnaabemowin: Namegos is trout; Michi Saagiig Nishnaabeg are Mississauga people, a branch of the Nishnaabeg nation living in the east; niibin is summer; Chi'Nibiish is the Mississauga name for Lake Ontario; kwezens (ikwezens) is a girl; Kokum is another name for Grandmother; jimaanan are canoes; semaa (asemaa) is tobacco; makizinan are moccasins.

20

THE ROCK ON
MISKWAADESI'S BACK

Nanabush gaa–giigoonyike. Nanabush was fishing, but he wasn't
catching any fish. He tried with his spear. He tried setting nets,
and he tried with a fishing pole. He put more semaa in the water. He tried at waabang, dawn. He tried at naawkwe, noon. He
tried at shkwaa-naawkwe, afternoon. He tried at dibikad, night.
No fish.

Nanabush was feeling frustrated and discouraged, and he was
getting very hungry. Just then, a little turtle popped out of a hole
in the rocks, but this was so long ago that turtles didn't yet have
shells. This turtle was just a body.

"Aaniin, Nanabush. You look sad. What's wrong?" asked
the turtle.

Nanabush explained the no-fish problem.

The turtle had an idea. "You know, Nanabush, I see lots of
fish in the rapids. Go and put your semaa down there and ask the
fish to come to you."

"Nahow," said Nanabush.

Nanabush paddled his jiimaan down to the rapids, put his
semaa down, and talked to the fish, and in no time he had all
the fish he needed.

"Miigwech, little turtle. You've really helped me, and, to
thank you, I am going to do something special for you."

Nanabush went and found a flat rock. He painted thirteen
sections on the rock, one for each full moon in the year. Then

he painted twenty-eight little sections around the edge of the rock, one for each day of the moon's cycle. He placed the rock on the turtle's back.

"Now you will always have a home. It's a home you can carry with you, and it's a home that will help the Nishnaabeg keep track of things. Your name will be Miiskwadesi, painted turtle."

Nishnaabemowin: gaa-giigoonyike—s/he was fishing; semaa is tobacco; wabaan is the morning; naakwe is noon; shkwaa-naakwe is afternoon; dibikad is night; jiimaan is canoe; and miiskwadesi is a painted turtle.

21

THE GIFT IS IN THE MAKING

In the old days, it was important to take care. It was important to nurture, and to love with all your heart. Nanabush taught us that one. Oowah. He used to walk all over, visiting with us, making sure we had enough food, water, medicine. Making sure our kids weren't sick. Making sure we were all getting along. Visiting. Why did we stop visiting?

One ziigwan, long time ago, that Nanabush is out visiting, walking all around Nishinaabe Aki, and he comes to the part in the east where the Mississauga live, where the Eagle, Crane, and Caribou clans live in the south. That part. And he comes to their place in the bush, where those ones live. He comes to visit. Oowah. It's a good thing to visit, to take care. It's a good thing to love.

He comes to that place where those Nishnaabeg live, and he can't find any of them there. No children. No fish smoking. Empty lodges. That Nanabush, he knows something is wrong, something is not right. It's ziigwan. The Nishnaabeg should be mending nets, setting nets, smoking fish. The ice is off the lake. The winter is in retreat. There should be woodpiles, fires, but, instead, there is nothing.

So, that Nanabush, he goes walking, looking for those Mississauga Nishnaabeg. He looks by the river. He looks by the lake. He looks in the bush by the rabbit trails. Nothing. He start to feel scared. He starts to feel real worried. Something is not right. The Nishnaabeg are missing. Nanabush's heart starts to rip open a bit. His heart starts to beat too fast.

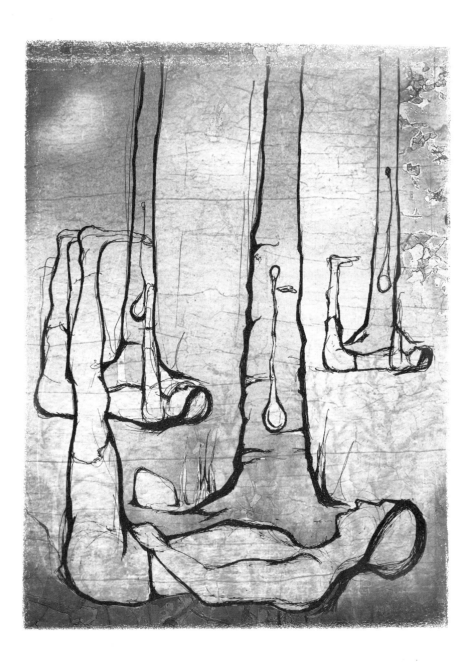

"Calm down," he tells himself. "Breathe."

He sits down and he thinks. He thinks about how much he loves those Nishnaabeg. How he doesn't see them enough. How, maybe, if he had just come earlier instead of spending so much time hunting with Ma'iingan, that this might not have happened. He feels really, really bad. He feels really, really bad in his heart, and his eyes make tears that run down his face onto the snowy ground.

Nanabush sits with that sad, and then he makes it into something else. "NISHNAABEG! NISHNAABEG!"

No answer.

"NISHNAABEG! NISHNAABEG!"

Silence.

Nanabush gets up onto his feet now, and he starts to do some thinking. He starts to do some walking, and he starts to do some more looking. And he looks for a long time.

Sometimes, in a story like this, Nanabush looks and right away he finds what he is looking for. But not this time. This time, he looks for a long time. A very, very long time.

After a few days, he sees something funny off in the distance amongst a stand of Ninaatigoog. He sees something, and at first he thinks he is seeing things from all the looking, but, as he get closer, he starts to understand. He sees brown feet and brown legs sticking straight up in the air. He gets closer. He sees brown back lying flat on the snowy ground in fact the snowy ground is kinda melty now, but brown back doesn't care. He gets closer. He sees a big mouth wide open. Like that big mouth is at the dentist.

But that big mouth is not at the dentist. She has ziiyaagmide dripping right in! That's right. This story takes place so long ago that our Ancestors did not have to make ziiyaagmide out of sap. Nope. The Ninaatigoog gave that syrup right out of their bodies, right over to whoever wants to drink it. And those Nishnaabeg, they always wanted to drink it.

Nanabush looks around the forest. Every tree is the same. Every tree has its own Nishnaabe, lying on his or her back, feet in the air with his or her mouth really, really wide open, and that maple syrup dripping right in.

"Bozhoo, Nishnaabeg!" yells Nanabush.

Nobody looks up. Nobody answers.

"Bozhoo, Nishnaabeg!" yells Nanabush.

Again, nobody looks up. Nobody answers.

"This is worse than I thought," thinks Nanabush. He gets an idea. He sings and dances and stomps and yells. But, nobody even notices.

Everybody is still flat on their backs, with their mouths really, really wide open with that ziiyagmide dripping right in.

Oowah, that ziiyagmide tastes good! That sweet brown syrup. That's the good stuff. Oowah.

But enough of that. This is a big problem, and Nanabush has to think up a big solution. And sometimes even Nanabush doesn't have any ideas. But he knows who does: Nokomis. That old lady will know what to do. That old lady will know how to solve this big problem. Those Nishnaabeg are going to get sick. They are not eating good food. They are not taking care of each other. They are getting weak just lying on their backs with their furry feet up in the air all day. They're getting soft in the mind, not thinking ahead, not looking ahead.

Everything is going to go in the wrong way if the Nishnaabeg get sick. Nanabush knows this. So he walks. He walks and walks and walks and walks. And finally he reaches Nokomis's house.

"Nokomis!" Nanabush yells. "NOKOMIS!"

"Holy!" that old lady says in response. "Why you yelling like that? Why you yelling like I'm not here?"

"Sorry," said Nanabush, giving her his semaa. He's not used to things being where they are suppose to be. But, this one, she where she suppose to be. He feels a bit better, and he sits by her fire in her lodge, and he explains his problem.

Nokomis just listens. And then she says, "Nahow. Aambe."

Nanabush is not quite sure what is going on. He was hoping for some medicine. He was hoping for a snack. Nokomis always has good snacks, or maybe a good story. Maybe a nap on that nice warm sleeping mat. Oowah. That is what he needs. Maybe some soup and that warm blanket wrapped around him. Sit by that fire. Get warm. Feel good. Oowah.

But here we go. "Aambe," that old lady say, and out the door she goes. Nanabush is not happy. His makazinan are wet. His feet are sore. He's been out walking for days. But out the door Nokomis goes, so out the door Nanabush goes.

Nokomis is an old lady, but she is fast, and she is strong, and she is all the way down the path by the time Nanabush gets out of the house.

"Bekaa!" yells Nanabush. "Wait." He thinks he hears her laughing under her breath, and she doesn't slow down. Nanabush has to pick up the pace a bit. His feet hurt. "Bekaa!" he yells again.

But Nokomis doesn't pay any attention. She's all the way down the path and around the corner. Nanabush is not happy, maybe he even starts crying a bit. Maybe he's feeling sorry for himself a bit. All this work. No one is paying attention to Nanabush. No one is taking care of Nanabush. But Nanabush doesn't have any time for feeling sorry.

"Aambe!" yells Nokomis.

So, Nanabush keeps walking. He goes around the corner, and Nokomis is standing at the bottom of Ninaatig, and she is already busy. She tells him to go to the south side of the tree and to make a hole. Nanabush does. She makes a spigot and attaches her akik. They hear the heartbeat of the liquid dripping into the bucket.

Beat. Beat.

Beat. Beat.

Beat. Beat.

Beat.

Nanabush feels better. Next, Nokomis tells Nanabush to taste the liquid, and Nanabush gets excited for that sweet, sweet taste of ziiyaagmide. Maybe he didn't get a fire, and maybe he didn't get any soup and that blanket, but, oowah, he is going to get ziiyagmide.

Except, when he dips his finger into that liquid, it isn't ziiyagmide.

"GAA GAAWIIN!" yells Nanabush. He can't take it any more. "This tastes like Nibiish."

Nokomis smiles a tricky smile. "Get a hold of yourself," she tells him. "Hang onto your shirt, young one. We're not done yet." She dips her cup into the akik and tells him to drink the sweet water, and then comes that big important part. This part is so important that those Nishinaabeg still do it today, even though everything nearly got all ruined.

Nokomis tells Nanabush that the sap, the ziisbaakdaaboo, is medicine, that it cleans us out. It cleans our bodies out for spring. "It's spring cleaning," she says, laughing under her breath. Zhaganosh thinks that means wash the curtains. Oowah. Washing your curtains don't clean out nothing. Drink ziisbaakdaaboo every day of Ziisbaakdooke Giizis. Then you'll be ready.

"Ready for what?" asks Nanabush.

"Ready for what happens next," says Nokomis.

Then she says, "Back to work," and she gets Nanabush to tap all the trees. She gets him to collect up all the dead wood and chop it into firewood. Then, she gets him to make a big fire. Nanabush is working so hard, he doesn't have time to feel sorry for himself. And makwag, amikwag, waawaashkeshiwag, all those animals help out. Soon everybody is busy, and that Nokomis is smiling a big smile.

And then she shows them how to concentrate that ziibaakdaaboo to save all its good for the niibin, and the dagwagin, and the next bboon. And they work hard with the fire and the stones, and finally they get their thirty buckets of ziibaakdaaboo down to one bucket of ziiyaagmide, and then finally they get it down to sugar.

And Nanabush is happy, because he's ready for a big party. After all that work, he knows Nokomis must have a big party up her old-lady sleeve.

But those old-lady sleeves are tricky, and Nokomis doesn't say anything about a party. She says, "Nahow, Nanabush. Back to the Nishnaabeg."

Nanabush's party face falls right off. He forgot all about those Nishnaabeg. And he doesn't have any solution to their problem, and they are far away.

And he needs a party.

"No party," says Nokomis.

He needs a party.

"NO PARTY," says Nokomis.

He was kind of looking forward to a party.

"Life is a party," says Nokomis. "Party down the trail and go make things right with the Nishnaabeg."

Nanabush knows when he been beat. So he party down the trail to go make things right with the Nishnaabeg. And he walks and walks and walks and walks, and he figures maybe those Nishnaabeg already got things all worked out. After all, how long could you lie on your back with your feet in the air?

Long time, if you're drinking maple syrup. Long time. Nanabush knows this because, by the time he gets back, the Nishnaabeg are still lying on their backs, feet in the air, mouths wide open. Drinking that maple syrup.

"Bozhoo, Nishnaabeg!" Nanabush yells.

Nobody pays any attention.

Nanabush figures he's got to get tricky at this point. Otherwise, he's going to have to do a whole bunch more walking, and he's never going to get any soup or blanket, and his feet are still wet. So he gets tricky. And he needs a bucket to get tricky. And he goes out to the river and fills up that bucket and climbs all the way to the top of Ninaatig, and he pours that bucket down the tree. He goes back and forth and he does this thirty times—one time for every day in Ziisbaakdaaboo Giizis.

And maybe that's how this story happened. Maybe. Maybe it was thirty buckets, or maybe Nanabush was way too tired to lug that heavy bucket up that tall Ninaatig. And maybe he is way, way too tired to do that thirty times. And maybe he has to go pee anyway. And maybe he decides to just whip it out when nobody is looking and do a big long thirty-bucket pee down the top of that tree. And maybe he saves himself thirty trips to the river and thirty trips up the tree, and he's a little closer to that soup and that blanket. Maybe it happened that way.

Whatever way it happened, by the time that "water" got filtered all the way through Ninaatig, and, by the time Nanabush did every tree in that sugar bush, the ziiyaagmide dripping into the mouths of Nishnaabeg wasn't ziiyagmide any more. It was more like Nibiish. It was more like tree pee.

Those Nishnaabeg noticed. And their mouths went shut, and their feet went back onto the ground, and they walked over to that Nanabush to find out what was going on. Now it was Nanabush's turn to be Nokomis. He told them he needed a big fire. They all got busy. He told them he needed a big stack of firewood. They all got busy. He told them he needed soup and a blanket and a foot rub.

They looked a little suspicious, but they all got busy.

Then Nanabush told them how much he loved them and how sad he felt when they forgot about the four sacred foods, and their responsibilities to each other and to the other clans. Nanabush drew them in close by the fire, and he told them how important they were. He told them how Gzhwe Manidoo had made them the most beautiful, caring creatures that ever walked the earth. He told them he wanted them to walk the earth a long, long time with them. He told them he needed them. He told them his heart knowledge, and they felt their hearts getting much, much bigger. They felt filled up.

The Nishnaabeg listened with their whole bodies. Then Nanabush took them to the south side of the tree, put his semaa down, and showed them how to tap the trees and collect the sap. He showed them how to cleanse themselves every day of Ziisbaakdaaboo Giizis. He showed them that, once the others found out what they were doing, everyone would come and help. He showed them how to boil that sweet water down into sweet sugar so they could keep that gift all year long.

The Nishnaabeg accepted that gift from Nanabush. And, every year, no matter how hard it is, they make sure their lips taste the sweetness of ziisbaakdaaboo, even if it is just once. Even if there isn't enough to make ziinzibaakwad, sugar. They take their kids. They tell the story of Nanabush. They listen for the heartbeat of their mother as that ziisbaakdaaboo falls into their pails. They cherish the gift given to their ancestors so long ago, and in their heart knowledge, hidden away in the most precious parts of their beings, they know that ziinzibaakwad wasn't the real gift. They know that the real gift was in the making, and that, without love, making just wasn't possible.

Nishnaabemowin: Ziigwan is the early part of spring; Nishnaabeg Aki is Ojibwe territory; ma'iingan is wolf; ninaatig is a maple tree; ninaatigoog means maple trees; ziiyaagmide is maple syrup; bozhoo means hello; Nokomis is Grandmother; semaa (asemaa) is tobacco; nahow means okay; ambe means come on! let's go!; makizinan are moccasins; bekaa means wait; akik is a pail; gaa and gaawiin both mean no; ziisbaakdaabook is sap; zhaganosh is a white person; Ziisbaakdooke-Giizis is March; makwag is bears; amikwag means beavers; waawaashkeshiwag is deer (plural); dawaagin is the fall; bboon is the winter; niibin is the summer; and Gzhwe Manidoo is the one that loves us unconditionally, the Creator; ziinzibaakwad is sugar.

ACKNOWLEDGMENTS

It takes a community of people to bring a book like this to print, and, first and foremost, I'd like to extend a chi'miigwech to countless generations of Nishnaabeg storytellers of all ages who have nurtured these stories, kept them alive, and passed them down through the generations during times when it was not safe to do so. It is a testament to their strength, commitment, and artistic integrity that these stories exist today. If I have imagined elements of these stories in a way that would offend my ancestors, I accept responsibility.

When I think back to some of my earliest memories of storytelling, I think of my extended family telling endless rounds of hilarious stories and jokes around kitchen tables and campfires. This was an excellent introduction into performance and storytelling, and the importance of laughter instilled in me a love of story.

My two children, Nishna and Minowewebeneshiinh Simpson, were the inspiration for this work, and miigwech to them for being my first audience, and for being very honest critics. This book would not exist without them. xo

A special miigwech to Gidigaa Migizi (Doug Williams). My telling of "Zhiingwaak Gets a Little Snippy" and "Gwezens Makes a Lovely Discovery" is influenced by his old-school, gentle style. I am very appreciative of his guidance and friendship, and it is always an honour to watch him transform a room or tipii full of people into a laughing mob of joyful souls! It is one of my very favourite sounds.

Three grandmothers—Edna Manitowabi, Marrie Mumford, and Shirley Williams—have supported and inspired this collection as well. Edna Manitwabi, a fantastic storyteller, performer, writer, and spiritual leader, taught me to be true to my own voice and my own heart. Marrie Mumford encouraged me to tell stories to children and for inviting me to perform many of these stories in the Nozhem First Peoples' Performance Space. Shirley Williams's knowledge of Nishnaabemowin in all its wonderful forms is simply expansive, and I thank her for always being willing to help me with the language. Any missteps, however, are my own.

The families of the Wii-Kendiming Nishinaabemowin Saswaansing listened to most of the stories in this collection from the fall of 2011 to the spring of 2012, and Vera Bell simultaneously translated them into Nishnaabemowin. Thanks to them for listening, acting out, drawing, and dancing these stories through the year with such exuberance. I hope that they continue telling their own versions to their parents, their children, their grandchildren, and their great-great-grandchildren.

Hilary Wear adapted and staged a site-specific production of "The Baagaataa'awe Game that Changed Everything" with a cast of local families on the winter solstice of 2011. Chi'miigwech to her for allowing me to witness first-hand the powerful combination of playfulness, children, and theatre. Chi'Miigwech to Wanda Nanibush and Patti Shaughnessy for noticing the storyteller in me, long before I noticed it in myself.

I sent the original manuscript to Niigaanwewidam James Sinclair on a whim. I had only envisioned photocopying the written versions of these stories for the families in the language nest. I am very thankful to him for his initial excitement and vision for the manuscript. I am grateful to him as an editor (the first Nishnaabe editor I've ever worked with) because his intimate cultural knowledge enabled him to see some of the old traditions of storytelling coming through, and the multi-dimensionality of the stories. Niigaan is a gifted storyteller himself, and his keen eye as an editor made this book come alive; it was an honour to work with a western-doorway Nishnaabe Inini. Thanks also to all the folks at Highwater Press for bringing this book into the world and including it within The Debwe Series.

Thank you to Amanda Strong for her moving interpretations of these stories through her illustrations.

Miigwech to Norbert Hardisty from Hollow Water First Nation for his assistance with the Anishinaabe word for Lake Winnipeg, Wiin nibii aang. Another way of saying it is "Wiin nibii gamik."

Miigwech to Steve, who has always been game for every single one of my ideas, through thick and thin.

This manuscript was completed in the Leighton Artist Colony at the Banff Centre with support from the Canada Council for the Arts and from the Ontario Arts Council.

An earlier version of "The Gift Is in the Making" was published in *Dancing on Our Turtle's Back* by Arbeiter Ring Publishing (Winnipeg, 2011) and is reprinted here with their permission.

The idea of lighting the seventh fire over again after it is blown out comes from Waawaate Fobister's play *Medicine Boy,* which I saw in Toronto as part of the Summerworks Festival in August 2012.

Chi'miigwech to Robert Houle for his always-enlightening and exciting conversations with me, but also for teaching me that birchbark biting is abstract art, as referenced in "Zhiingwak Gets a Little Snippy."

The word and concept of Gwiingwa'aage in "Honouring Ojiig in the Night Sky" is from Tobasanokwut Kinew, quoted in Michael Wassegijig Price's "Anishinaabe Star Knowledge" (*Winds of Change,* 2002 17[3]: 51-56).

Makizinkwe comes from the dictionary *Indinawemaaganidog—All My Relations: Anishinaabe Guide to Animals, Birds, Fish, Reptiles, Insects and Plants,* published by the Great Lakes Indian Fish and Wildlife Commission, Odenah, Wisconsin, for the Anishinaabeg words for *lady's slipper* (49) and *jewelweed* (79). I have also consulted Richard A. Rhodes's *Eastern Ojibwa-Chippewa-Ottawa Dictionary* (Mouton de Gruyter: New York, 1993) throughout the book, particularly the Curve Lake dialect. I have also used the *Ojibwe People's Dictionary*, available online at <http://ojibwe.lib.umn.edu/>. I learned the word *kipimoojikewin* from Maya Chacaby's thesis, *Kipimoojikewin: Articulating Anishinaabe Pedagogy Through Anishinaabemowin Revitalization* (University of Toronto, 2011). Miigwech, Maya, for this important work.

FURTHER READING

Caduto, Michael J., and Joseph Bruchac. *Keepers of Life: Discovering Plants Through Native American Stories and Earth Activities for Children.* Golden, CO: Fulcrum Publishing, 1994.

Caduto, Michael J., and Joseph Bruchac. *Keepers of the Earth: North American Stories and Environmental Activities.* Golden, CO: Fulcrum Publishing, 1988.

Coatsworth, Emerson, and David Coatsworth (comp). *The Adventures of Nanabush: Ojibway Indian Stories.* Toronto, ON: Doubleday, 1979.

Cook, Connie Brummel. *Maple Moon.* Markham, ON: Fitzhenry and Whiteside, 2006.

Benton-Banai, Eddie. *The Mishomis Book.* Hayward, WI: Indian Country Communications, 1988.

Gaikesheyongai, Sally. *The Seven Fires: An Ojibway Prophecy.* Toronto, ON: Sister Vision Press, 1994.

The Great Ball Game: A Muskogee Story. Retold by Joseph Bruchac. New York, NY: Dial Books for Young Readers, 1994.

Johnston, Basil. *Living in Harmony.* The Anishinaubaemowin Series. Cape Croker, ON: Kegedonce Press, 2011.

Johnson, Patronella. *Tales of Nokomis.* Toronto, ON: Stoddard Kids, 1994.

Johnston, Basil. *Ojibway Heritage: The Ceremonies, Rituals, Songs, Dances, Prayers and Legends of the Ojibway.* Toronto, ON: Royal Ontario Museum, 1976.

Johnston, Basil. *Tales the Elders Told: Ojibway Legends.* Toronto, ON: Royal Ontario Museum, 1981.

Lunge-Larsen, Lise, and Marci Preus. *The Legend of the Lady Slipper: An Ojibwe Tale*. Boston, MA: Houghton Mifflin, 1999.

McLellan, Joe. *The Nanabosho Series*. Winnipeg, MB: Pemmican Publishing. <http://www.joemclellan.ca/books.htm>

Nish Tales: Walking and Talking with Nanbush. <http://nanabush.ca/>

Odjig, Daphne. *The Nanabush Series*. Odjig Arts, 2011 [1971].

Ojibwe Cultural Foundation. *Gechi-Piitzijig Dbaajmowag: The Stories of Our Elders*. Ojibwe Cultural Foundation, 2011.

Peacock, Thomas, and Marlene Wisuri. *The Good Path*. Afton, MN: Afton Historical Society, 2002.

Reid, Dorothy M. *Tales of Nanabozho*. Toronto, ON: Oxford University Press, 1963.

Stories from the Seventh Fire: The Four Seasons—Traditional Legends for Each Season. Kelowna, BC: Filmwest Associates, nd.

Treuer, Anton, et al. *Awesiinyensag: Dibaajimowinan Ji-gikinoo'amaageng*. Minneapolis, MN: Wiigwass Press, 2012.